WELCOME TO DWEEB CLUB

Also by Betsy Uhrig

Double the Danger and Zero Zucchini
The Polter-Ghost Problem

WELCOME TO DWEEB CLUB

Betsy Uhrig

MARGARET K. MCELDERRY BOOKS

New York   London   Toronto   Sydney   New Delhi

MARGARET K. McELDERRY BOOKS
An imprint of Simon & Schuster Children's Publishing Division
1230 Avenue of the Americas, New York, New York 10020

This book is a work of fiction. Any references to historical events, real people, or real places are used fictitiously. Other names, characters, places, and events are products of the author's imagination, and any resemblance to actual events or places or persons, living or dead, is entirely coincidental.

Text © 2021 by Betsy Uhrig
Cover illustration © 2021 by Lisa K. Weber
Cover design by Debra Sfetsios-Conover © 2021 by Simon & Schuster, Inc.

MARGARET K. McELDERRY BOOKS is a trademark of Simon & Schuster, Inc.
For information about special discounts for bulk purchases, please contact Simon & Schuster Special Sales at 1-866-506-1949 or business@simonandschuster.com.
The Simon & Schuster Speakers Bureau can bring authors to your live event. For more information or to book an event, contact the Simon & Schuster Speakers Bureau at 1-866-248-3049 or visit our website at www.simonspeakers.com.
Also available in a Margaret K. McElderry Books hardcover edition
Interior design by Irene Metaxatos
The text for this book was set in Excelsior LT Std.
Manufactured in the United States of America
0722 OFF
First Margaret K. McElderry Books paperback edition August 2022
10 9 8 7 6 5 4 3 2 1
The Library of Congress has cataloged the hardcover edition as follows:
Library of Congress Cataloging-in-Publication Data
Names: Uhrig, Betsy, author.
Title: Welcome to Dweeb Club / Betsy Uhrig.
Description: First edition. | New York : Margaret K. McElderry Books, [2021] | Audience: Ages 8-12 | Audience: Grades 7-9 | Summary: Jason Sloane and his seventh-grade friends are the first to sign up for a strange new club that monitors school security footage, but when the new computers show the club members themselves as unlikable high school seniors five years in the future, they scramble to solve the mystery.
Identifiers: LCCN 2021010324 (print) | LCCN 2021010325 (ebook)
ISBN 9781534467682 (hardcover) | ISBN 9781534467699 (paperback) | ISBN 9781534467705 (ebook)
Subjects: CYAC: Mystery and detective stories. | Future life--Fiction.
Classification: LCC PZ7.1.U3 We 2021 (print) | LCC PZ7.1.U3 (ebook) | DDC [Fic]--dc23
LC record available at https://lccn.loc.gov/2021010324
LC ebook record available at https://lccn.loc.gov/2021010325)

For Lisa: Through thick and thin
and seventh grade

WELCOME TO DWEEB CLUB

Chapter

THE ORIGINS OF THE FLOUNDER BAY UPPER SCHOOL H.A.I.R. Club are shrouded in mystery. Or maybe cloaked in mystery. Or at least wearing a heavy cardigan of mystery. As the official club historian, I tried to figure it out, and you can decide whether I was at all successful. I do know one thing, though: None of us would have joined if Glamorous Steve hadn't gotten there first. And if we hadn't joined, our lives would have turned out very differently. I'm not just saying this for dramatic effect—it is a fact.

But let's start at the beginning. A history should go in order, after all.

It was the second week of seventh grade. I was still finding my way around the building, which was way bigger and more crowded than elementary school, and mentally labeling kids I didn't know (Vegan Lunch, Stork Legs, British Accent, et cetera). When I walked into school that morning, there were folding tables lining both sides of the main hall. The tables had posters hanging in front of them advertising various school clubs. Two or three upbeat kids who looked way too cheerful for that time of day sat behind each table.

All these upbeat kids were trying to get other, lower-beat kids to join their clubs, offering enticements like mini-muffins, and those rubber bracelets that really hurt if you shot them at people, and even tiny Frisbees with FBUS ULTIMATE FRISDEE (oops) printed on them.

It was my intention to walk right by these tables and keep going until I got to my locker. It was not my intention to sign up for a club that morning. I like to take my time making big decisions, and joining a school club was a big decision. Your choice of clubs could determine a whole new set of friends and also what kinds of labels would get slapped on *you*. It was way too early—in the day and the year—for me to be making a decision with these kinds of life-changing consequences.

But I didn't make it to my locker. My friend Glamorous Steve was standing at the last table in the row, and he grabbed the strap of my backpack as I was hurrying past, causing me to lurch to a stop.

"Jason," he said. "Wait up."

"What?"

"I'm going to sign up for"—he looked down at the sheet

of paper that was the only thing on the table—"H.A.I.R. Club. You should too."

No one, upbeat or not, was sitting behind the table. There were no posters. There was no swag. There was a sign-up sheet with a coffee ring on it and *New This Year! See Ms. Grossman, Faculty Adviser, for Details!* scrawled across the bottom in red pen. Ms. Grossman was my US History teacher, and even this early in the year, I was all too familiar with her red scrawls.

"Is this a joke?" I said. I glanced at the sheet with its un-filled-in blanks. There wasn't even a crummy pencil next to it. "There's no one signed up at all. And what is Hair Club, anyway?"

"It's not Hair Club," said Steve. "It's H.A.I.R. Club. It's initials."

"So what do the initials stand for?"

"No idea. Maybe 'Hair And Its Relatives'?"

I could see why that might interest Steve. He had perfect hair and he put real effort into its upkeep. It did not, however, interest me and my normal-to-greasy, effort-free hair.

"So it *is* Hair Club," I said. "And what's a hair relative? Fingernails? Sorry. Not interested."

I had turned to head for my locker when Steve put a hand on my shoulder.

"Here's the thing," he said. "Whatever it stands for— and it might have nothing to do with hair—H.A.I.R. Club is brand-new. No one is signed up yet. We'd be the first members."

I shrugged his hand off my shoulder. But I turned back to face him. "So?"

"So if we join now, as seventh graders, we'll be club officers by the time we're in, like, eighth grade."

Now he had my attention.

"If we're the first to sign up," I said, thinking out loud, "wouldn't we be club officers right away? It's only fair."

Steve was nodding at my brilliant logic. Or maybe at my willingness to go along with him. He handed me a pen. "We'd be in charge of a brand-new club. In seventh grade. Think about it," he said.

I was already signing my name.

A word about Glamorous Steve before we go on. Steve's family had moved to Flounder Bay the summer before sixth grade. There are three kinds of new kids, as I'm sure you know. There's the weird new kid, the bland new kid, and the glamorous new kid.

Steve, who was from California and had that perfect hair and a smile that pretty much made a cartoon twinkly *ping* whenever he flashed it, was as glamorous as it got in Flounder Bay. His glamour was upped by the fact that a hopelessly bland kid also named Steve had moved to town at the same time. So there was Steve and there was Glamorous Steve. And then, for most of us, there was just Glamorous Steve, the other kid having been forgotten. Or maybe he changed his name. Doesn't matter. He won't appear in this history again.

Glamorous Steve had a talent for doing even the geekiest things with such infectious enthusiasm that he made them not just acceptable but downright trendy. He was a long-distance runner. Boring, you say? Yes, indeed. Unless Glamorous Steve was moving effortlessly past you, his glorious hair streaming behind him. He collected stamps. Game over, you're thinking. And ordinarily you'd be right. But he made it work. Somehow, he made it work.

So I knew I was safe signing up for anything Steve was a part of. In fact, even as Steve was writing his name below mine on the H.A.I.R. Club sign-up sheet, his glamour was rippling through the hallway and other kids were falling into line behind him. They didn't care what he was signing up for—if Glamorous Steve was in, they wanted in too.

I should add that fully half of them balked when they got to the point of actually writing their names. After all, they had no idea what H.A.I.R. stood for. And they could see for themselves the empty table and its pathetic sign-up sheet. Even Steve's glamour wasn't enough for them to risk their reputations on what looked like the losingest club ever. I don't blame them. And I'm glad only ten kids signed up.

Those others will never know what they missed.

chapter

2

THE FIRST-EVER MEETING OF THE FLOUNDER BAY
Upper School H.A.I.R. Club took place on September 9, a
Tuesday, at three o'clock in the afternoon. Eleven people
were present, and I'm going to describe each of them
briefly, since almost all of them have a major part in this
history.

First, there was Ms. Grossman: history teacher and
club adviser. She had a big vocabulary and a mean red pen
and wasn't afraid to use either.

Next, Jason Sloan: me—your narrator. I hate those scenes
in books where the poor narrator tries to describe what they
see in a mirror and point out their flaws to seem humble. I
was extremely ordinary, kind of scrawny, often mistaken for
a sixth grader when I was in seventh. Will that do?

"Glamorous" Steve Hendricks: who has already been introduced. I don't think he needs any more description.

Nikhil Singh: a friend of Steve's from cross-country. I sat behind Nikhil in history, so I was familiar with the unusual angle at which his ears attached to his head. I also knew that he was easily irritated, based on his grouching about my "tuneless humming" during quizzes.

Harriet "Hoppy" Hopkins: daughter of the owners of Hopkins Hairnets, the second-biggest company in Flounder Bay. Hoppy was noticeable around school for her ultra-curly hair, which would have driven her hairnet-manufacturing ancestors up a wall, and her, um, commanding voice.

Andrew Vernicky: the tall redheaded boy from my science class whose laid-back attitude almost covered up how smart he was. He never raised his hand, but when he was called on, he was always right. He once corrected the teacher.

Sonia Patel: possibly the most agreeable person I'd ever encountered. Even her outfits were agreeable. She managed to color-coordinate her backpack and shoes with her clothes every day. Sonia had huge brown eyes and always wore a (matching) hairband in her dark brown hair.

Laura Andersen: the shy blond girl from my math class. I swear I'd met clams that were more outgoing than Laura was.

Vincent Chen: How do you describe your best friend since kindergarten? Vincent had messy black hair and a goofy smile. Good enough? He had joined all the school's clubs on a dare from his older sister. Vincent never could resist a dare, something I myself occasionally took advantage of.

Two other kids whose names I never found out. Their descriptions aren't important, for reasons I'll get to later.

The interesting thing to note here is that all the club members were seventh graders. Coincidence? Not really.

At Flounder Bay Upper School, seventh through twelfth grades are in one building together because the town is too small to need separate ones. This meant that any kid who was older than seventh grade already knew about the school's clubs and wouldn't have bothered with that lone H.A.I.R. table at the end of the row. They knew what clubs they wanted to join, and they joined them.

In fact, Vincent could have gotten away with not signing up for H.A.I.R. Club, because his sister had no idea it existed. But Vincent has a strong code of honor. Plus, I made him.

Anyway, back to the first meeting . . .

Ms. Grossman started things off.

"Welcome to H.A.I.R. Club," she said, trying to sound enthusiastic in the face of this small and skeptical-looking group. "This is the first year that Flounder Bay Upper School has offered H.A.I.R. Club, and I'm so glad you've decided to join!" You could hear her tossing in that exclamation point with effort. "I'm Ms. Grossman, as those of you who are my US History students know. And I am your club adviser. Which is awkward, because I have to admit that I have no idea what H.A.I.R. stands for.

"Here's the backstory," Ms. Grossman went on, taking a seat on the edge of the desk at the front of the room. "This past summer, a very successful entrepreneur who wishes to remain anonymous offered the services of his company to install a state-of-the-art security system here. He very generously donated this to the school with one stipulation."

Ms. Grossman, I knew from being in her class, constantly used words like "entrepreneur" and "stipulation" without defining them. When someone asked what one of her words meant, she'd tell them to "write it down and look it up—you'll learn it better that way." I tended not to bother, which might explain the number of red corrections on my papers.

"That stipulation," Ms. Grossman continued, "was that we start a club here at school called H.A.I.R. Club, and that its members take charge of the security system."

Now we were all sort of eyeing one another.

"Ha!" barked Ms. Grossman. "I see some questions on your faces. And maybe the first one is, who in their right mind would put a student club in charge of a brand-new state-of-the-art security system? The same thing occurred to me. But the donor was quite clear about it. Club members *only* will monitor the system." She raised a finger and added, "Which might be a good thing, because I don't think any of the adults here could even begin to figure it out."

One of the nameless kids raised his hand.

"Yes?" said Ms. Grossman.

"So this club doesn't have anything to do with hair?" he asked.

"No, it doesn't," Ms. Grossman said. "H.A.I.R. must stand for something, but the donor never indicated what it was."

The kid who'd asked the question stood up, along with the girl next to him.

"We thought H.A.I.R. spelled *hair*," the girl said as they headed for the door.

"Well, it does, of course," said Ms. Grossman. "Although in this case—"

But they'd already opened the door. The girl practically dove into the hallway. The boy lingered long enough to look around and say quietly, "'Welcome to Dweeb Club' is more like it" before he made his escape. I think I was the only one who heard him, since I was nearest the door.

Okay, so this new club involved security cameras and computer equipment. But that didn't make it Dweeb Club just because some chucklehead said so. Did it? This wasn't a roomful of dweebs. We had Glamorous Steve and . . . and . . .

Uh-oh. What had I gotten myself into?

chapter 3

"OKAY," SAID MS. GROSSMAN. "I CAN CERTAINLY UNDER-
stand the confusion. Did anyone else think this was a hair
club?"

"I did," Hoppy said. "Since my family's in the hairnet
business, I thought I'd join to do some opposition research.
But state-of-the-art security sounds interesting."

I looked at Steve. So did most of the other kids in the
room. He was the main reason we were here, after all. He
ran a hand carefully through his own hair as though asking
it a question. A question like *Is it okay if I join a club that
isn't devoted to you and your relatives?* I guess the answer
was yes, because he said, "I thought it might be about hair,
but I'm good either way."

"Excellent," said Ms. Grossman. "And the rest of you
are still on board?"

Everyone else nodded. I hesitated for a moment. Now was the time to get out if I was going to. I could follow the nameless girl and boy out into the hallway, leaving Steve and Vincent and the rest to Dweeb Club. But I couldn't do that. Vincent and Steve were my best and second-best friends. Besides, however dweeby this might turn out to be, it was already better than Hair And Its Relatives. I nodded. Not that anyone had been waiting breathlessly for my approval.

"I'll leave the rest to you, then," said Ms. Grossman. "Today you need to elect your club officers: president, vice president, treasurer, and secretary. You meet Tuesdays and Thursdays, so on Thursday I'll show you the equipment. Got it?"

We all nodded again.

"All righty. See you then."

And she was out of there as if she had somewhere better to be.

"Okay," Steve said as soon as Ms. Grossman was gone. "Let's elect some officers." He smiled, knowing he was about to be elected H.A.I.R. Club president in a landslide.

But he wasn't counting on the ambitions of one Jason Sloan, who wasn't an athlete or a stamp collector or a naturally good student. I needed this more than he did.

I cleared my throat. "Maybe we should go by who signed up first," I said. "Wouldn't that be the fair thing to do?"

Steve's smile remained in place. "That's an interesting idea, Jason. Though if we were going to take it in that direction, why not start with whoever was at the table first?"

He had me there.

"I think we should vote," said Hoppy. "Otherwise aren't we just basing it on whoever got to school earliest yesterday? How is that fair?"

She had me there too.

My whole idea was ridiculous and I knew it. "Okay," I said. "Let's vote."

We all looked around expectantly. And we all came to the same conclusion at the same time: We had no idea how to start voting for club officers.

"Are we supposed to *run for office*?" Vincent said, like he was asking if we were supposed to eat live grubs.

"That seems like a waste of time," said Hoppy. "Let's just vote for who we want for each position."

"But what if someone ends up getting elected who doesn't want to be?" said Laura in a voice barely above a whisper. As soon as she'd spoken, she retreated back behind her protective curtains of blond hair.

"How about this," said Steve, already showing leadership skills. "Anyone who *doesn't* want to be an officer, raise your hand."

Laura's hand went up first, followed by Vincent's and Andrew's.

"Okay," Steve said. "Now you can choose who you want to be president from the rest of us."

He grinned again as if he expected we were going to rise up and cry out in unison, "Steve is our president and king!" No one did that, obviously.

"Oh, for pete's sake," Hoppy said when Steve's grin started to go stale. "We have to vote anonymously. Hand me some blank sheets of paper and a ruler."

"Coming right up," said Sonia, though it wasn't clear Hoppy had been speaking to anyone in particular. Sonia extracted a turquoise notebook from her turquoise backpack and tore out a couple of sheets of paper. She opened a turquoise pencil case and handed Hoppy a ruler.

Hoppy tore the paper into strips using the ruler and handed them out. "For each position, you write a name on the slip. Got it?"

"Good plan," said Steve, trying to reclaim some authority. "But we need to put the slips in something when we vote, right?" He looked around for a container.

"Here," said Hoppy, fishing around in her backpack. She held out to Steve an object that looked like a large dust bunny.

"Gross," said Steve, not taking it.

"It's a hairnet," said Hoppy.

Steve still wasn't buying.

"I've never worn it," Hoppy added. "It's a sample."

"Okay. But you hold it," said Steve, showing admirable skill at compromising.

I could have written my own name on my slip, but what was the point? Steve was the better candidate. I got one vote, and I'm sure it was Vincent's. All the others went to Steve.

There followed the votes for vice president (Hoppy), treasurer (Nikhil), and secretary (Sonia). I voted for myself for each of these, but clearly our new democracy was already broken. When the votes for secretary had been tallied and Sonia declared the winner, it became embarrassingly obvious who the one person was who hadn't taken his name out of the pool and yet hadn't been elected to an office.

I was starting to wish I had curtains of hair like Laura's to hide behind when Steve (already an awesome president, I'll just say it) broke the excruciating silence.

"You know what?" he said. "I think we need a club historian too. I mean, this is the first year for a new club. We need a record."

"Isn't that the secretary's job?" the traitorous Vincent asked.

"The secretary records the minutes of the meetings," said Hoppy.

"I have no idea what that means," said Sonia, club secretary.

"You write down what we talk about at the meetings and what we decide," Hoppy explained.

"How do you even know that?" Andrew asked for all of us.

Hoppy shrugged. "Hopkins Hairnets is a family company. I go to some board meetings."

"So what would a historian do, I mean, theoretically?" I asked as casually as I could.

"The historian would keep a written history of what happens to the club," said Steve.

"And that's different from what we decide?" I asked.

"It definitely is," said Hoppy. "Believe me."

So that's the tragic tale of how I wanted to be the president of the Flounder Bay Upper School H.A.I.R. Club and ended up the historian—a pity position invented especially for me.

What follows is the historian's account of how the club's first year turned out to be way more interesting than any of us could ever have expected.

chapter

I WAS IN MY ROOM THAT EVENING, TYPING THE FIRST pages of H.A.I.R. Club official history, which mostly meant playing around with fonts, when my aunt and uncle arrived at the house. They lived nearby and came over for dinner a lot.

Uncle Luke is my mother's baby brother, as she still calls him and apparently always will. His wife, Shannon, is my cool aunt, or at least I thought she was until that night.

We sat around the table after dinner, eating dessert and waiting for Uncle Luke to do his missing-tooth trick with a glob of brownie. This trick was a favorite of my sister Alice's. She was six and had some missing teeth herself.

In the meantime, Shannon asked me how seventh grade was going. My parents perked up here, because I hadn't told them anything and they were probably afraid

I was some kind of outcast who'd spent the first days of school inside his own locker, dangling from a hook by his underpants.

"It's okay," I said.

At this my parents perked back down, because it was the response they were used to already.

"Have you joined any clubs?" Shannon asked.

I was a little annoyed by her question, because hadn't she skipped right over asking me if I'd gone out for any sports? I thought about telling her I'd gone out for football, just to see if she'd do a spit take with her coffee.

"Why do we have to keep talking about Jason?" Alice whined. "I'm sick of talking about Jason and his new school."

"We talked about your school last year," said my mother. "Remember? When it was new. This year Jason's school is new."

"But my new school was Jason's old school," Alice said.

"Alice," said my dad in his first-and-only-warning voice. "Leave it."

"I was actually voted the official historian for a club today," I said to Shannon.

"Awesome," said Shannon. "Which club?"

"Dork Club," said Alice, using her favorite word for anything involving me.

"It isn't Dork Club," I said, though I couldn't be totally sure of that. "It's H.A.I.R. Club."

"That's not a real club," said Alice. "It's just letters."

"Of course it's a real club," said Shannon. "The letters must stand for something. Sounds mysterious and intriguing to me."

Alice looked a bit ill. How was it possible that her cool aunt could be interested in something her dork brother was doing? I may have looked surprised myself, for the same reason. I mean, Shannon had tattoos around her upper arms and wore T-shirts and sneakers to work.

"H.A.I.R.," said Alice, who was learning to spell, "spells 'dork.'" Not that she was good at it. She was, however, very good at hijacking a conversation. Especially one focused on me.

"No, it doesn't, honey," my mom said to her. "It spells 'hair.' The *h* sound is 'hah'—"

"Clubs are for dorks," Alice declared.

"I was in the computer club in school," said Shannon, who probably meant to contradict Alice, though her example wasn't the best.

"You are such a nerd!" Luke said affectionately.

"No, she's not," said Alice. "She has tattoos."

"Don't let those fool you, kid," said Luke. "You know what those tattoos are around her arms?"

It turned out none of us did.

"Tell them, hon," said Luke.

"They're the runes from the dwarves' map in *The Hobbit*," said Shannon.

"*The Hobbit* isn't nerdy," said Alice, who only knew it

from the movies she wasn't allowed to watch.

"Oh-ho, yes, it is," said Luke. "Those tattoos basically mean 'I'm a gigantic nerd' in Dwarvish. They're like a beacon for fellow geeks."

"Worked on you, didn't it?" said Shannon, punching his arm.

Cool Aunt Shannon was a nerd. A cool nerd, maybe? Was there such a thing? At what point did her nerd side overtake her cool side? This was actually an interesting question, but now was not the time for it. Luke was doing his brownie-glob thing.

chapter 5

THE EIGHT REMAINING H.A.I.R. CLUB MEMBERS
gathered on Thursday in the classroom where the first
meeting had taken place, then Ms. Grossman walked us
downstairs to the school's basement.

"The equipment is set up in an unused janitors' closet
down here," she explained as we descended.

I'm pretty sure I wasn't the only one thinking along
the lines of *Great, not only are we in the losingest club
ever, but they've stuck us in a closet in the basement.* No
one said anything, though, and this was probably due to
the fact that it was sort of interesting being allowed in
the basement, which was ordinarily off-limits to students.

All kinds of stuff lurked down there: ancient gym
equipment that looked like it had been used for jousting
in the Middle Ages, giant rusty kitchen appliances that

looked like they should have been thrown out, bags and bags of that sand they throw over puke on the floor, and enough shovels and brooms and pitchforks to equip a good-size angry mob.

We went past a couple of janitors' closets that were in use and ended up at the last one on the hall: H.A.I.R. Club headquarters.

"Gross," said Hoppy as we squeezed inside.

"Awesome," said Andrew at the same time.

It was both. A smallish room with barely enough space for nine of us. Two metal desks. Two rolling chairs with janitor-butt imprints in them. A buzzing fluorescent light overhead. It was like the interrogation room in a very-low-budget cop show. All of this is what made it gross.

What made it awesome outweighed those things. On the desks were two slender laptop computers that looked like they came from a *Star Trek* set. Not the older TV shows, not the movies. The new streaming TV shows you have to pay for. On one wall was a bank of nine cardboard-thin big-screen monitors. This equipment looked like an advanced alien civilization had left it here to shame our backward technology.

The monitor screens were blank until Ms. Grossman powered up one of the laptops, and then they all brightened at once. We oohed and aahed as if she'd lit up a giant holiday display, even though the screens showed our school, which was boring enough when it wasn't almost empty, which it was now.

Eight screens showed a different area: four sides of the exterior of the school, the cafeteria, the main hallway and the upstairs hallway, and the lobby outside the office. The scenes weren't static; they shifted slowly so you could see different angles. Ms. Grossman tapped the laptop, and sound came from invisible speakers on the screens.

"Each screen has its own volume setting," she said, "so you don't have to listen to them all at once." She lowered the volume on each of them, one at a time, until there was silence again. "Eight of the screens show what's happening live," she said. "But the cameras are also recording twenty-four seven, so you can play back anything from any time on the laptops or on the ninth screen. Neat, huh?"

We nodded, even though no one besides Ms. Grossman would have used the word "neat" to describe anything in this room. Or anything ever.

"And that's about the extent of my knowledge of this system," Ms. Grossman admitted. "The donor said you'd be able to figure out the rest using the onscreen prompts."

She looked at her watch. "One more thing," she said. "This goes without saying, but I'm saying it anyway. This is a security system. If we did have a security issue, the authorities here at school and even the police would have priority access to it. But no one is monitoring it on a regular basis except you. So if you see something that you think someone in authority should know about, you need to tell me or the office immediately. Understood?"

"Understood," President Steve said for all of us.

"And also," Ms. Grossman went on, "if you see or learn something that might embarrass someone but is in no way a security issue?"

She paused for the idea of this to sink in. It did. Possibilities that no one had even considered popped up in our imaginations.

"It doesn't leave this room," Ms. Grossman concluded. "And if you're not sure where to draw that line, you come to me. Got it? If any of you abuses the trust we've put in you by giving you access to this system, you will be out of the club first and quite possibly in a lot more trouble after that. Understood?"

"Understood," Steve repeated.

"Excellent," said Ms. Grossman. "Take good care of this stuff. Make sure you're out of here by four, and don't forget to lock up." And she left the office, closing the door behind her.

chapter

AS SOON AS MS. GROSSMAN WAS GONE, THERE WAS A
mad rush for the laptops. Andrew and Nikhil got there first
and had managed to sit down before Steve held up a hand.

"Wait," he said. "Before we get started . . ."

"Yes?" said Nikhil when the pause had gone on for too
long.

Steve's eyes widened and he concluded: "Is this stuff
amazing or what?"

"It's very amazing," said Hoppy. "But isn't it also
weird?"

"It is weird," said Andrew, looking at the screen in
front of him. "This is *not* a normal laptop."

"Not that," said Hoppy. "Or, not only that. I mean,
isn't it weird that the school is basically giving a bunch of
seventh graders access to everything that goes on here?"

She walked over to the big screen showing the main hall, where a few kids were wandering around. She turned up the sound using a bar on the side. We could hear Stork Legs and Saxophone Case arguing about whose mother they should call for a ride home.

"Yeah," said Vincent, "but it's giving us access to the most boring place in the known universe: this school."

"Plus," said Nikhil, still concentrating on the screen in front of him, "whoever set this up has thought of all that. Take a look."

We crowded around, jostling for a view of the screen in front of him. "Read All Legal Provisions Header (R.A.L.P.H.)," it said at the top, with a lot of tiny print underneath.

"It's one of those user agreements," said Nikhil. "The kind you usually just scroll over and agree to without reading it?"

"Yeah," said Vincent. "So keep scrolling."

"It won't let you," said Nikhil. "I already tried. You have to read it."

"How does it know?" asked Sonia.

"It must somehow scan your eyeballs," said Andrew from behind his screen.

"Does it hurt?" asked Sonia.

"My eyes! My eyes!" Nikhil croaked dramatically and unhelpfully.

"Cut it out," Steve said. "It doesn't hurt," he assured Sonia. "Does it?" he asked Andrew.

"No. Can't feel a thing."

We took turns reading the agreement and signing our lives away. We basically had to promise to forfeit our entire futures if we used anything we learned from the system recordings for "personal gain" or to "injure or discomfit another party or parties." It went on and on about "discretion" and "ethical behavior."

My eyes were so glazed by the time I was done with the "Nondisclosure of Overtly Proprietary Equipment (N.O.P.E.)" clause that I'm surprised the computer was able to tell I'd read the last few paragraphs, which were about not telling anyone outside the club how the equipment worked. But somehow it knew. It wouldn't let Vincent sign off until he'd gone back over a section that he admitted he had skimmed.

"Check this out," said Vincent when he was finally done. He turned the laptop around so more of us could see it. "It took our pictures while we were reading and made profiles for us."

"I look awful," said Sonia, who was sitting at the other laptop. "The puke green of the wall in the background clashes with my shirt. Can I retake mine?"

We all looked awful in our pictures because we'd been reading something boring when they were taken without our knowledge or consent. We looked slack-jawed and glassy-eyed. Even Glamorous Steve's photo looked like a late-night mug shot.

We hunted desperately for a way to retake the pictures,

with no luck. It was Laura who noticed the tiny print under them.

"It says," she reported in a voice so quiet we had to lean in toward her, "'This photograph will be disseminated as widely as possible under Broadcasting of Unflattering Reading Photographs (B.U.R.P.) protocol in the event of any perceived breach of the user agreement by the above-pictured individual.'"

"Fiendishly clever," said Andrew. "So if we mess up and break the agreement we just signed, these pictures will be all over the Internet."

"It can't do that," Nikhil scoffed. "How would it even know?"

"You don't think so?" said Hoppy. "You can be the first to test it, then."

Nikhil chose not to test it, then or ever. The rest of us never even considered it.

"All right!" Vincent announced after a moment. "We're in."

A new screen had opened up with the company name and what was apparently its motto:

WELCOME TO PRESCIENT SECURITY SYSTEMS
YOUR FUTURE IS SAFE WITH US

"As long as we don't breach the user agreement," I said. "If we do that, our future is totally ruined, am I right?"

chapter

7

NIKHIL AND ANDREW WERE BACK BEHIND THE LAPTOPS, learning their way around.

"Watch this," said Andrew, pointing at the big screen showing the front of the building. We watched as he made the focus zoom in on three kids sitting on a bench outside the main doors. He zoomed and he zoomed until we were way past a close-up and inside the left nostril of the kid in the middle.

"Gross," said Hoppy.

"Awesome," said Vincent at the same time.

It was both. With the focus that close, the audio had zoomed in too—we could hear the air whooshing in and out of the kid's nose.

"I'm thinking deviated septum," said Andrew.

"Maybe allergies," said Sonia.

"Too bad there isn't more going on at this time of day," said Nikhil, who'd been moving around other locations on the other screens while we listened to Deviated Septum's nose whistle.

There was general nodding until Steve remembered an important fact: "It's recording twenty-four seven, though, isn't it?" he said. "Doesn't that mean we can watch what happened earlier too?"

"Yup," said Andrew. He started punching away at the laptop like someone in the midst of a red alert in a sci-fi movie. "Here we go: Archives."

The ninth screen, which had been blank, lit up. It showed the main hall too, only now it was full of kids. The time stamp in the corner indicated that school was about to start—this morning.

"Look!" said Steve. "There I am."

Sure enough, Steve, who had a locker in the main hall, was coming toward the camera.

"Don't you dare go up my nose," he warned, but it was too late—Andrew was already there.

"Wow," said Sonia quietly.

Even the inside of Steve's nose was perfect.

We zoomed back out, and Nikhil appeared onscreen opposite Steve.

"Do my ears really look like that from behind?" Nikhil asked.

I, for one, knew that they did.

"Like what?" Sonia asked.

"I don't know," said Nikhil. "Handles."

"Or a radar array," Vincent put in.

"I can't believe we're using this super-duper security system to monitor our own ear placement," said Andrew.

"I can't believe you used the word 'super-duper,'" said Nikhil.

"I think 'super-duper' is two words," said Hoppy.

This got no response because it didn't deserve one.

"Ms. Grossman said we should lock up at four," said Steve. "What time is it?"

"It's three fifty-seven," said Andrew, consulting the laptop screen.

So we turned off the monitors and shut down the laptops. Then we filed out of the janitors' closet and Steve locked the door behind us.

"So is H.A.I.R. Club totally cool or totally boring?" Vincent asked.

This got no response because none of us had one.

chapter

8

"HOW WAS DORK CLUB, DOOFUS?" ALICE ASKED WHEN I got home that afternoon.

"You know," I said, "a dork and a doofus aren't the same thing."

"But you are one," said Alice.

"I am what?" Why did I engage with her? Why?

"A dork *and* a doofus. You're a dorkus!" Alice cackled at her own joke. "You're a dookus. You're a dookie!"

"Mom!"

But Mom wasn't home. My parents own the bookstore in town (Flounder Bay Books—I know, original), and Mom, who usually got home before Alice did, had stayed late because someone was out sick.

Uncle Luke, who had one of those jobs you can do in your pajamas from home, was in the kitchen making lasagna. Uncle Luke made really good lasagna, even when he put spinach in it, as he was now. Tons of it.

"It cooks down!" he said when he saw my expression.

At around six, Aunt Shannon pulled up to the house in her little convertible (something that definitely went on the cool side of her cool/nerd equation).

"Here's my ride," said Luke. "We'll just hang out until your parents get home."

Aunt Shannon was wearing her usual work outfit: jeans, sneakers, and obscure-band T-shirt. Shannon worked for Woozle, the biggest company in Flounder Bay, which was way bigger than the second-biggest company, Hopkins Hairnets. Hopkins Hairnets had been the only company in town until Woozle came along ten years ago.

Woozle is the giant Internet search engine entirely for medical issues. I bet your parents have used it when you got a Lego stuck up your nose or something like that. Aunt Shannon described Woozle as "Google for hypochondriacs." (I'm not going to make you "write it down and look it up": a hypochondriac is a person who worries constantly about their health.)

The company has a huge building on the outskirts of town. The building is surrounded by a "campus" with walking trails and even a golf course. They have their own softball field too, but even so, the Hopkins Hornets always beat the Woozle Warthogs at corporate softball. There's way more muscle power among the hairnet makers.

Luke wandered back into the kitchen, and Shannon asked me how H.A.I.R. Club was going. I described the security system and the user agreement and the embarrassing ID photos, being ultra-careful not to go into enough detail to activate B.U.R.P.

"So what does 'H.A.I.R.' stand for?" she asked.

"No idea," I said. "It must have something to do with security."

Shannon pulled out her phone. "What's the name of the company that made the equipment?" she asked. "We can have a look at their website—unless you guys already did that?"

We hadn't. In our defense, we'd run out of time. In our non-defense, I'm not sure we would have bothered anyway.

"Hmm," said Shannon after some fast poking. "Are you sure you have the name right?"

"Prescient Technologies," I said. Then I spelled "prescient" for her.

She rolled her eyes. More poking.

"Nothing," she said. "That's strange. You'd think a company making high-tech stuff like that would have a web presence. Very strange."

I agreed that it was strange, because I guess it was. I mean, if even the company that ships your bananas has a web address printed on the little banana stickers, you'd think a security company would have one. Maybe they were so secretive and mysterious they didn't want a website. Maybe they did most of their work for governments and reclusive billionaires and didn't want just anyone knowing about them.

But this led to an unavoidable question: Why give such cutting-edge equipment to Flounder Bay Upper School for free?

I was about to run this past Shannon, but then Mom and Dad came home and lasagna-heating directions were discussed, and Luke and Shannon were leaving.

As they pulled away in the little convertible, Alice cornered my parents in the kitchen.

"Jason called me a dookie," she said.

chapter
9

TUESDAY'S H.A.I.R. CLUB MEETING WAS FAIRLY TAME.
Hoppy insisted we set up a chart for taking turns with
the equipment. Nikhil objected, Sonia tried to compromise, and Steve decreed we'd start using the chart
on Thursday. (For the record, it was never mentioned
again.) Nikhil and Steve then spent most of the hour following their cross-country assistant coach, Mr. Bradley,
around because they suspected he went outside to smoke
between classes. He was indeed sneaking out. To eat
Twizzlers.

I noticed that Sonia was taking secretary notes, so
I decided I needed to take historian notes too. When I
couldn't find a pen in the mess in my backpack, I asked
Sonia if I could borrow one. Unfortunately for me, she
was wearing a blouse with yellow pom-pom fringe. I felt

like a fool writing my official-historian notes using a pen with a yellow pom-pom bobbing on top.

On Thursday, we got our first actual security assignment.

"So Ms. Wu called me down to the office today," Steve said when we'd assembled in our headquarters.

"What'd you *do*?" asked Sonia, aghast.

Ms. Wu was the vice principal—the school enforcer. None of us had had any direct experience with her, but we already knew enough to fear the call-down.

Steve chuckled. "I didn't do anything," he said. "There's been a security breach. She wants us to look into it."

"Have they called the cops?" asked Andrew.

"We don't need any cops," said Vincent.

"*Cops?*" said Nikhil. "We're not cheesy TV criminals."

"No need for officers of the law," said Steve. "Ms. Meager in the cafeteria says something got into the croutons overnight and she wants to know what it was."

"As in, what kind of animal it was?" Hoppy asked.

"Correct."

"Those croutons are always stale," said Vincent. "I don't know why an animal would breach security to eat them."

Laura was already signed on. She brought up the recording of the cafeteria from last night and put it on the big screen so we could all see it.

"What time?" she asked.

"Try after dark," said Steve. "Whatever it was is probably nocturnal."

"Plus, it doesn't mind staleness," Vincent added.

"I'll start at nine," said Laura.

She focused on the kitchen, where the giant vats of food were stored. We watched as nothing happened for a few minutes.

"Can we speed it up?" asked Hoppy.

Laura did, and the nothing started happening more quickly.

"Faster," said Nikhil.

High-speed nothing.

"That's as fast as it goes," said Laura.

"Wait!" said Sonia. "Pause for a sec."

Laura paused.

"Now back up. . . . Keep going. . . . There! See it?"

Laura let the recording move forward, but slowly.

"What exactly are we looking for?" said Hoppy.

"Like a blur or something. Over by the door," said Sonia.

It was Hoppy who confirmed the sighting. "There," she said. "Near the door to the cafeteria. Something's moving."

Laura backed the recording up again and then moved the view into the cafeteria itself. Then she let it play forward. And that's when we all saw it.

"That's one giant raccoon," said Vincent. "And it's walking upright."

chapter
10

IT WASN'T A GIANT RACCOON WALKING UPRIGHT. IT was a person. No, it was a whole crowd of people. In the cafeteria of the Flounder Bay Upper School. At five past midnight.

"Was there some kind of event here last night? A PTO meeting?" Hoppy asked.

We watched the action on the screen for a moment.

"Those aren't grown-ups," said Steve. "They're kids."

They were. Older than we were—high schoolers, definitely—but kids.

"Maybe some kind of really popular club met here last night," said Andrew.

"Not possible," said Vincent. "I'm a member of every club at this school. There were no club meetings last night. And no club is that popular. Look at all those kids."

The cafeteria was full. In fact, it seemed like a typical lunchtime crowd.

"They're eating," said Laura. "This must be a recording from lunch. I must have pulled the recording for twelve noon, not twelve midnight. Sorry." She fiddled with the laptop.

"Okay, the time stamp says twelve a.m.," Laura said as she let the recording play.

"It's showing the same thing as before," I said.

We watched the impossible twelve a.m. lunch period go on for a while.

"Move over to the windows," said Hoppy.

Laura shifted the angle some, but the windows remained out of view. "This isn't working as well as usual," she said. "I can't zoom around easily."

"Try right-clicking," said Andrew. "That always does something."

"Right-clicking does not always—" Nikhil began.

"Oh, here it is," said Laura.

"All hail the right-click!" said Vincent.

"I have to pick a view," said Laura. "That's weird."

The angle shifted abruptly and we were looking at the windows.

"See?" said Hoppy. "It's daylight outside."

"At midnight?" said Nikhil. "Something is way messed up. Let me do it." He elbowed Laura out from behind the laptop.

Nikhil poked around for a while, and the recording

lurched forward and backward, making me a little motion sick.

"This has to be it," he said finally, and he let the recording move forward again at 12:15 a.m.

"Still lunchtime," I said. "The time stamp must be wrong. It should be p.m."

"Who eats at twelve p.m.?" asked Hoppy.

"Seniors," said Vincent.

"I don't recognize anyone there," said Sonia.

"Maybe that's because you don't know any seniors," said Nikhil.

"I know lots of seniors," said Sonia. "My brother is a senior. And I don't see him or any of his friends."

"I'm thinking ghosts," said Vincent. "Ghosts of kids past who meet at midnight to enact—"

Nikhil didn't let him finish. *"Ghosts?"* he said. "This isn't *Scooby-Doo*."

"They do seem a little out of focus," Sonia said carefully. Then she waited for the avalanche of ridicule.

"She's right," said Steve. "Try zooming in," he said to Nikhil.

Nikhil zoomed jerkily in on a kid no one recognized. The image got bigger but remained fuzzy. Nothing like the sharp image of the Twizzler flecks in Mr. Bradley's teeth from last time.

"I can't get any closer," said Nikhil. "And don't say it—I already tried right-clicking."

"Okay, zoom out, way out," said Steve.

"Yes, sir," Nikhil snarked, but he did it.

The image was still out of focus.

"Plus, there's no sound on this recording," said Nikhil. "The volume is all the way up."

We listened to the silence and watched the fuzzy strangers eat their fuzzy lunches.

Andrew sat down heavily on a desk.

"Are you okay?" Sonia asked him.

Andrew didn't answer at first; he kept studying the ninth monitor with its view of the lunch scene.

"Here's the thing," he said after a moment. "I keep telling myself it's not what I'm seeing, but I think it is. Do you guys see it?"

"What?" asked Hoppy. "See what?"

"Me," said Andrew. "Over there by the drink machine. I see me."

chapter

11

IT'S WORTH EMPHASIZING HERE THAT ANDREW
Vernicky wasn't just tall for his (our) age. Which he was.
He was tall for *any* age. He was a head taller than any
other seventh grader and right up there with the tallest
high schoolers. People were always asking him if he played
basketball, which he did not.

His hands were distinctive as well—graceful, with the
kind of long fingers piano teachers swoon over. He didn't
play piano either. Andrew was a constant source of frus-
tration to piano teachers and basketball coaches through-
out Flounder Bay.

"Are you sure that's you?" asked Vincent.

"Who else could it be?" said Andrew. "Those are definitely my hands." They were. "And my hair." It was. "And
that's my UC Santa Barbara sweatshirt."

A UC Anything sweatshirt was rare in the hinterlands of Flounder Bay, so we all stared as Nikhil focused on the sweatshirt.

"It must have shrunk in the wash," said Andrew. "Darn. I love that sweatshirt."

The sleeves were definitely too short, making Andrew's hands even more noticeable. And the person at the drink machine was definitely Andrew. Except—

"You look different," said Steve.

"Even taller," said Hoppy.

"Have you been working out?" Sonia asked.

We studied onscreen Andrew. He did look different. He looked bigger all over, especially in the shoulder region. We turned to live Andrew and his shoulders in particular. No change. He shrugged the shoulders in question.

"No," he said. "Not lately."

"So what were you doing in the cafeteria at midnight?" asked Vincent.

"I think we've determined that this recording doesn't show the cafeteria at midnight," Hoppy said. "It's clearly daylight."

"I eat at ten thirty, with you guys," Andrew said. "And who are these other kids?"

Nikhil started moving the focus around to the various kids, closing in on their faces.

"Well, there's Hoppy," he said finally, pausing on a figure standing beside a table toward the center of the room. The table, I should add, that Hoppy always sat at.

"Oh my god," said Hoppy. "That is me." She paused for a few seconds. "Sort of."

"You've got boobs," said Sonia, her voice tinged with awe.

Hoppy, who was short and had that wild head of hair, looked almost exactly the same onscreen. The main difference was the one Sonia had just mentioned.

Hoppy looked down at her chest. That seemed to give everyone else permission to do the same. It did not match the one onscreen.

"Okay," she said. "I didn't look like that earlier today. And I wasn't in the cafeteria at midnight *or* noon."

"It's obvious what's going on here," said Steve.

"Is it?" I asked.

"Sure. There's something wrong with this so-called state-of-the-art security system. The thing is broken."

"That does explain it," Sonia threw in.

"No, it doesn't," I said. "It doesn't explain it at all. If there were something wrong with the system, it might leave out chunks of time or record the same thing over and over. But it wouldn't put some of us in the cafeteria when we weren't there and make us look . . . um . . . bigger," I said, going for a word that covered both Andrew's and Hoppy's situations.

"Maybe," said Andrew, "the program is somehow mashing different times together. Maybe it's been recording over itself, so different lunchtimes are layered on top of each other. Maybe that's my head on someone else's body. And also my hands."

"That's got to be what happened to me," said Hoppy.

"But is that your sweatshirt on someone else's body?" I asked Andrew.

"Maybe?"

Andrew's explanation made better sense than any others we could think of, but it didn't seem like enough of an explanation.

"It's a working theory, anyway," Steve said presidentially. "It's past four," he added. "We've got to finish up."

We shut down the laptops and the monitors, and Steve locked the door behind us. "Let's try to have a few more theories on Tuesday," he said. "We'll figure it out."

"We didn't even figure out what was eating the croutons," said Vincent.

chapter 12

THAT NIGHT I DIDN'T HAVE TIME FOR WORKING THEO-
ries. I had a lot of homework, and Alice decided to perform
one of her "shows." This had been happening more and
more since Alice had spent the summer at kids' theater
camp being told she had a "talent for drama." Which she
definitely did. Just not the way the camp counselors probably meant it.

"Tonight," she announced right after dinner, "for a
limited time only, I, Alice Sloan, present a special presentation of my sold-out show—"

"Alice," said my father in his get-on-with-it tone of
voice.

"Oh boy, a show!" said Mom, having a seat on the
sofa. "Come on, Jason." She patted the cushion next to
her.

"I've got a ton of homework," I said, truthfully but not regretfully.

"It'll just take a minute," said Mom.

"No, it won't," said Alice. "This is a feature-length show."

"You've got five minutes," said Dad.

I plopped down next to Mom as Alice took her position in the middle of the living room rug. Dad remained standing, eyeing his watch.

"Tonight's show is *The Ugly Dorkling*," she announced.

"Oh, for pete's sa—" I began.

"Quiet in the audience," said Alice. "The show is about two normal parents who have a son who is an ugly dorkling. And he doesn't grow up to be a swan. He grows up to be a big, big dork. And he joins the Dork Club at his stupid new school and . . ."

She went on for exactly five minutes, snapping at us to "keep watching me" when we dared look away. Then my dad shut her down.

The "show" itself never started—she just described the "plot," which didn't amount to much except the terrible things that happened to her thinly disguised main character. By the time "the beautiful and smart princess swan, Alicia" was born to the overjoyed parents, even my mom had stopped chuckling appreciatively.

I escaped to my homework while my parents lectured Alice on how words could sometimes be hurtful.

You may be asking what all this has to do with the history of H.A.I.R. Club, and the answer is not much. Except don't dramatic scenes and conversations make history "come alive," as Ms. Grossman would say? Even if it's just me, my parents, and my deranged little sister involved?

Although I should say here that if you're looking for things like character development and poetic descriptions, you are barking up the wrong book. If you want that type of stuff, go to Flounder Bay Books (shameless plug), and find yourself something good to read.

Chapter 13

THE NEXT CLUB MEETING FOUND US DIVIDED. STEVE was leading a faction that included Sonia and Nikhil and possibly Laura (hard to tell) that felt like we should get to the bottom of the Crouton Critter Mystery before we went on to solve the Twelve A.M. Lunch Mystery. The rest of us wanted to go back to the midnight recording and figure out what was going on.

Things got a little intense until Steve and Hoppy settled on a compromise: We would pull up the recording from last night at midnight, which could show the Crouton Critter but might show another impossible lunchtime scene.

As before, we sped through a lot of nothing happening in the cafeteria until around 10:30 p.m., when something flashed by.

I was at the controls, and I wasn't used to them, so I

was annoying everyone with how slowly I was responding to their commands. I couldn't get the recording to pause until past eleven, then I had to back up while my colleagues made personal remarks and Nikhil told me to put a sock in the tuneless humming.

Finally, I stopped at ten fifteen and went forward again in slow motion. No kids in the cafeteria, but yes— from out of the kitchen came an animal. It was dark in there, so we had a hard time identifying the creature at first.

"Is that a raccoon?" said Vincent.

"Too small," said Nikhil.

"Maybe it's a possum," said Laura.

"No way is it a possum," I scoffed. "It's a cat."

"Cats don't eat croutons," said Hoppy.

"Guys," said Steve. "Come on. You're ignoring the obvious because you don't want it to be true."

He was right. By this time I'd frozen the image onscreen and was zooming in. It wasn't a cat—it was a skunk.

"Ew!" said Sonia.

"So why doesn't it stink in the cafeteria every morning, if a skunk's been there?" Vincent asked.

"Because no one's been bothering it," said Andrew. "They don't spray unless you bother them."

"Let's see where it goes and then we can move on to more important things," said Hoppy.

I inched the recording forward to the point where the skunk left the cafeteria, then lost it.

"You have to switch views to the hallway," said Nikhil, elbowing me aside. "I'll do it."

He took over and followed the skunk out of the cafeteria and into the hallway, where it roamed around as if it owned the place, which was disturbing. What if it decided to make a nest and have babies in my locker some night?

Nikhil couldn't keep up with the skunk either, though. He lost it when it went into the girls' locker room. The girls were horrified, so they must have been worried about the thing making a nest in their gym clothes, but there was nothing more we could do.

"Mystery solved?" said Steve hopefully.

"Not really," I said. "We don't know how it's getting in."

"Good enough for today?" Steve asked.

"Sure."

We moved on to more important things.

Hoppy took over for Nikhil at the laptop, and she was no better than I was, but somehow there were fewer remarks.

She brought us right up to the brink of midnight and then hesitated.

"Go on!" said Vincent.

"I'm afraid of what we might see," Hoppy admitted.

"Like, aliens with giant exposed brains or something?" Vincent asked.

"No. Like nothing. Like last time was a glitch and now it's normal."

"And we have a year of checking up on Stinky

McSkunk the Crouton Crook," said Andrew. "And nothing else."

We all backed off. Some of us literally took a step away from Hoppy.

"Whenever you're ready," Steve said quietly.

chapter
14

HOPPY LET THE RECORDING MOVE FORWARD AT normal speed, and this is what we saw on the ninth screen: dark, empty cafeteria. More dark, empty cafeteria. And then, as the time indicator in the corner went from 11:59:59 to midnight, the room lit up. It was like Dorothy stepping out of the gray house and into Technicolor Oz. Suddenly the cafeteria was bright and full of kids. They didn't trickle in from the hallway—they were already there.

"Whoa," said Steve. "Do that again."

"Do what again?" said Hoppy. "I didn't do anything."

"Go from eleven fifty-nine to twelve o'clock again."

She did, and the same thing happened: empty and dark to full and light in the span of a second.

"Cool," said Vincent.

"That's impossible," said Nikhil. "They can't just

appear there like that. There's something massively wrong with this thing."

"Obviously," said Hoppy. "Either there's something wrong with it or the Flounder Bay Upper School cafeteria is magic."

We let that idea dangle there for a moment, during which I'm sure we all came to the same conclusion: The Flounder Bay Upper School cafeteria was not magic.

"There I am again," said Andrew, pointing to the screen.

"And there I am," said Hoppy.

Both were still larger onscreen than off.

"Pan around," said Steve to Hoppy. "Let's see if we can find anyone else we know."

She started moving closer to one face after another. I was pretty sure I saw a kid from Spanish I had labeled "Destined for Piercings" go by.

"Wait," said Nikhil. "Is that me?"

It was the back of some kid's head. Some kid with ears like handles. Nikhil's ears. His hair was longer than Nikhil's, though. Hoppy kept the focus on him, and we waited for him to turn around.

"Good lord," muttered Vincent when he did.

It was Nikhil, all right. But he had a mustache. A thin, sad-looking mustache. We gaped in horror. Until we got a good look at the kid next to him.

"No," moaned Steve softly. "No, no, no, please, no."

But yes. It was Glamorous Steve. Or formerly glamorous Steve.

"What is wrong with my *hair*?" Steve practically wailed.

Steve looked taller onscreen, but it was the hair that really stood out. Or no longer stood out. Steve's floppy, perfect hair was shorter and . . . it's hard to describe. It looked both lumpy and flatter, as if someone had made a cheap Steve doll with molded-plastic hair.

"Look away!" said Steve. "Look away!"

But Hoppy was closing in relentlessly.

"That's as good as it gets," she said. The close-up was fuzzy, just as the midnight images had been last time. "I can't get any more detail."

"Is it a wig?" Sonia asked tentatively.

"It better be," said Steve.

"Maybe it's part of a costume," said Sonia. "Like for a play or something."

Steve just shook his head. Theater wasn't his thing.

"Could be product of some kind," said Vincent. "Some type of off-brand gel . . ."

Steve was nodding now. "That has to be it," he said.

Hoppy finally had mercy on Steve and moved away from him and his hair. We located Sonia after a good amount of scanning around the room. She was in a corner, vigorously making out with some kid none of us recognized. It took a while for us to convince the real Sonia, when her onscreen version came up for air, that she was looking at herself.

"My parents say I can't date until after I'm married,"

she half joked when she'd finally admitted what we were seeing. "And did I trip and take a header into the discount-makeup bin?" The onscreen Sonia had definitely gone a little overboard with the makeup. Her eyes were already big, but onscreen they looked manga size. "Are those *false eyelashes*?" she wondered aloud.

"Actually," said Hoppy, "I think the kid you're going at it with is wearing even more makeup than you are." He was. Then Hoppy spoke for all of us when she said, "Is it me or does it look better on him?"

Sonia groaned. "That pirate blouse we're both wearing looks better on him too. Where would a person even shop for a thing like that?"

Vincent was hard to spot for a different reason: We found him slumped over a table, his head resting on a pile of books.

"I think I'm asleep," he said when he'd examined himself. "It's possible I'm drooling."

"Keep moving," I said to Hoppy as she pulled away from Vincent, leaving him to his nap. "I want to find myself. If everyone else is there, I must be too."

Hoppy panned the cafeteria for a while, but I was not to be found.

"We're almost out of time," Steve said.

"Fast-forward," I told Hoppy.

"You're not going to see yourself in a blur," Hoppy objected, but she did it anyway. We watched kids quickly eating, chatting, throwing out trash, leaving for class.

Hoppy was right. No one's face was recognizable at this speed. The room emptied out. Then, when the time stamp went to 1:00:00 a.m., the bright and empty cafeteria turned dark and empty. We were in the present again.

"Huh," said Hoppy. "So the weird midnight lunch scene lasts exactly an hour."

"Back up a bit," I said. "So we can watch everyone leave at normal speed."

Now she was just indulging me, and everyone knew it, but we watched a few minutes of kids exiting the cafeteria. We saw Vincent, among the last of them, stagger out with his pile of books. No Jason.

Which was strange. Shouldn't I have been with Vincent at lunch? We always sat together. And, come to think of it, shouldn't Steve have been sitting with us too?

When Steve moved to Flounder Bay the summer before last, the first kid he met here was his neighbor Vincent. Which meant that the second person he met was me. So Steve started hanging out with us before he realized how glamorous he was for Flounder Bay and that he could easily do better than Vincent and me. By the time school started, it was too late—we were friends. The three of us had sat together at lunch ever since.

"Oh well," I said. "We can look for me again next time."

We shut everything down and locked up.

And if you've noticed that we never found or even bothered to look for Laura, congratulations. I certainly didn't.

chapter
15

THAT NIGHT WE HAD ENDURED TWO "ACTS" OF ALICE'S new show, *Make Way for Dorklings*, when the house phone rang. I sprang up to answer it—something I never did ordinarily. Anything to get away from the inept Mr. (Jason, obviously) Dork leading his little dorklings directly into traffic while heroic Officer Alice tried to save them.

It was Vincent. He was calling on the landline because the school had a rule against students having cell phones until ninth grade, and our parents—unlike anyone else's we knew of—actually obeyed that rule.

"The plan's a go for tomorrow night," Vincent said in an unnecessarily secretive tone.

"Um, I'm not sure I'm going to be able to—"

"You already said you would."

"But my parents—"

"No problem. It's all arranged. You're invited to my house for dinner and to 'work on a H.A.I.R. Club project,' quote unquote," Vincent said. "You 'might have to stay overnight if we don't finish,' quote unquote."

"Stop saying 'quote unquote,' quote unquote," I said.

"Good one," said Vincent.

"Okay, I guess," I said.

"Excellent," said Vincent.

So the plan was a go. Which was not what I was expecting when I'd agreed to it, to be honest.

Vincent and I had been walking home after H.A.I.R. Club when Steve jogged up behind us.

He wasn't at all out of breath when he caught up to us. "I have an idea," he said.

We kept walking as he talked.

"I was dropping off the H.A.I.R. key in the office," Steve said. "And nobody was there."

"So?" said Vincent.

"So when I put the key on the hook, I noticed a bunch of other keys hanging there."

"And?" I said.

"And I took one."

"Which one?" Vincent asked. Which wasn't *my* first question.

"Gym, outer door," said Steve.

"Isn't someone going to notice it missing?" I said.

"Unlikely," said Steve. "There are at least five copies of

every key. Seriously, someone in the office must have been locked out a lot as a kid and never gotten over it."

Because one of us had to, I asked, "Why did you want the key to a gym door, anyway?"

"Because I think we need to find out what really goes on in the cafeteria at midnight," said Steve.

I was more confused now. "You think something really happens in there at midnight?" I said. "That it's not a glitch or recording error or whatever?" I paused for breath and to gather my thoughts into semicoherent form, then continued. "You think that there's some type of . . . I don't know . . . alternate world where weird versions of us eat lunch in there at midnight? Is that it?"

I thought all this had been withering, but Steve just shrugged. "Maybe," he said. "It's worth checking out, right?"

"Of course it is," said Vincent.

"We can't sneak into the school at midnight," I said at the same time.

"Why not?" said Steve. "I have a key."

"Because we'll get caught," I said, with a huge "duh" in my voice.

"By one of our many trained security guards?" said Steve.

"No. By the security cameras. The state-of-the-art security cameras positioned around the school." But even as I spoke, I was realizing how dumb this objection was.

"And who is in charge of monitoring those security cameras?" Steve asked triumphantly.

"Ha!" said Vincent.

"My parents will never let me out of the house at midnight," I said. "And neither will yours." This last remark was aimed mainly at Steve. Vincent and I both had siblings to soak up excess parental attention. But Steve was an only child, and the scrutiny was intense. The three of us referred to Steve's parents as the Eye of Sauron.

"We can figure something out," said Steve.

We'd halted at the corner of my street. Steve and Vincent lived a couple of blocks away.

"Fine," I said, not meaning it.

"I'll call tonight with the deets," said Vincent.

They had walked away before I could warn him never to use the word "deets" in my presence again.

If you think my mom and dad would object to my staying overnight at Vincent's on a school night, you haven't met Vincent's parents. My parents knew full well that I'd probably be in bed before my usual bedtime and that I'd have brushed and flossed thoroughly too.

What my parents didn't know was that Vincent's parents cared a lot about the quality of their sleep. They had a white-noise machine in their bedroom and used those puffy sleep masks to keep out any stray photon of light. Which meant that when they were asleep, they stayed that way.

Vincent's sister, Karen, was never seen without her earbuds in and spent virtually all her time at home in her room. She wouldn't be an obstacle either.

Of course, without obstacles, my mind was free to explore the possibilities of breaking into the school at midnight and finding . . . what, exactly? . . . in the cafeteria.

First I had to worry about the breaking-in part. If we were caught, it would go on our permanent records, which would easily cancel out any points we'd score by being club officers in seventh grade. They'd probably disband the H.A.I.R. Club altogether because students couldn't be trusted with monitoring school security.

And then where would I be, a voice in my head squeaked anxiously. H.A.I.R. Club was already turning out to be way more interesting than that empty table in the main hall had first hinted. And without it I'd instantly go from Historian for Mysterious New Club That Definitely Isn't Dweeb Club right down to Random Seventh Grader with No Obvious Attributes. And very few friends.

Finally, as I lay in bed later that night, the worry that came creeping to the front of my mind while these other, more rational ones lurked at the back was the one about meeting up with some alternate version of myself and the others in the cafeteria at midnight. That never goes well in science fiction, does it?

chapter 16

SO, DINNER AT VINCENT'S . . . FIRST, VINCENT'S parents are both really good cooks. But since they are even better hosts, they didn't bother to cook for me. They ordered pizza.

Karen was forced to remove her earbuds at the table, so she took the opportunity to torment her younger brother. (And if you're wondering, yes, it was part of our bond that Vincent and I were both tormented by our sisters. In fact, we were both tormented by each other's sister too.)

"So you guys are in H.A.I.R. Club together?" Karen asked me by way of opening a stealth attack on Vincent.

"Um, yeah."

"Are you in any other clubs, Jason?"

"Um, no, just H.A.I.R."

"Huh. Vincent is in a lot of clubs, aren't you, Vinnie?"

Vincent hated being called Vinnie, as I'm sure I don't need to tell you.

"Yep," said Vincent. "A lot of clubs."

"That's got to be hard to manage along with your schoolwork, and don't forget Chinese school on the weekends," said Karen. She shook her head sadly at her brother's poor life choices.

Vincent's parents' antennae rose at this. Vincent hadn't told them that he'd joined every club in school on a dare from Karen.

"I'm doing fine."

"Sure you are," said Karen. "And how's Crochet Club?"

The muscles around Vincent's jaw started to flex even though he was not currently chewing on anything. "Great, actually. I'm the vice president."

He hadn't told me that. Was it impressive? Unclear. It was Crochet Club, after all.

Vincent's parents looked impressed, anyway, and Karen couldn't allow that.

"So it's you and a group of girls sitting around crocheting?"

"Not at all," Vincent said. "Olaf Olaffson is a member. And he's really good. He's been teaching me a ton."

Olaf was a kid from Iceland who barely spoke English.

"So it's you and Olaf and a group of girls?"

"No."

Karen did the math. "You and Olaf are the only

65

members, aren't you?" She made another calculation. "Which makes him club president."

"So?" said Vincent.

Karen just laughed. But Vincent would have his revenge. I'd already seen the hat he was crocheting for her.

We were in bed, thoroughly brushed and flossed, at nine thirty. But we had our clothes on. Vincent set the alarm for eleven fifteen in case we fell asleep.

Which we did. When the alarm buzzed, Vincent pressed the snooze button and rolled over. When I poked him, he whined, "Just a couple more minutes," so I was forced to poke him harder.

"Ow!"

"Sorry. We have to go. Steve's waiting outside."

I could see the gloss of his hair below the window, under the streetlight.

Vincent flopped out of bed and put on his sneakers. We grabbed flashlights, Vincent took a house key, and we moved silently (except for that one creaky step) downstairs and out the front door.

"How'd you escape?" Vincent asked Steve.

"I told my parents I needed their help with my math homework," said Steve.

"And they bought it?" Steve didn't need help with his math homework. Ever.

"They were flattered but totally out of their depth. I kept saying I didn't get it until way past their bedtime.

They were practically crying when I finally let them go. They'd sleep through a meteor strike now."

The three of us didn't discuss why we were going where we were going. Or how potentially stupid our plan was. We just talked about how strange it was to be walking to school in the dark with no one else around.

The school looked downright eerie when we got there. It wasn't totally dark, because of the security lights, but the vaporish white glow only made it look more like the first scene in a horror movie. Like vampires, we shunned the lights, keeping to the shadows as we crept around to the back, where the door to the gym was.

Steve slid the key into the lock, and the door opened easily—to my disappointment, I admit. We slipped through the doorway one by one, then paused. The big clock behind the protective cage on the gym wall said 11:40.

"Perfect timing," said Steve. "Right?"

"Um, sure," I said.

Vincent didn't answer. He kept glancing around like something with rows of needle-sharp teeth was about to lunge for his throat. "I'm going to turn on my flashlight," he said.

"We don't need it," said Steve.

We really didn't. There were security lights in the gym and in the hallway beyond.

"I just don't like all these shadows and dark areas," said Vincent. "I feel like the ghosts of kids who were bullied in gym are hovering nearby."

If you're thinking he had an overactive imagination, keep in mind that we were there with the specific purpose of finding out if alternate versions of ourselves somehow sprang to life at midnight in the cafeteria. So why not the ghosts of kids targeted in ancient games of dodgeball dodging vengefully around in the gym?

Steve and I switched on our flashlights without comment, and the three of us made our way toward the hallway, sneakers squeaking loudly on the shiny floor. We were out in the hall, halfway to the cafeteria, when we heard a voice from somewhere ahead of us.

"Hey!" it yelled. "Where do you kids think you're going?"

Chapter 17

GYM GHOSTS? CAFETERIA GHOULS? ACTUAL SECURITY guards that we weren't aware the school had? Did it matter, really?

We froze.

Then three figures emerged from the cafeteria.

If we hadn't already been frozen, we would have then.

Steve had the presence of mind to shine his flashlight at the figures as they came toward us.

"Is it them?" whispered Vincent.

"Who?"

"The other us."

"You boys are in so much trouble," one of the figures said loudly. It was the shorter, curly-haired one. The other two laughed.

"Ohmygod," said Vincent as the three got closer, "it's the other girls."

More laughter. "We're not the other us," said Hoppy. "We're the us-us."

And if you know what she meant by that, you're way ahead of where Steve, Vincent, and I were at that point.

"Huh?" said Steve, speaking for me and Vincent as well. Then, when he'd gotten up to speed: "What are you three doing here?"

"Sonia has this theory about the kids in the cafeteria at midnight," said Hoppy. She sighed. "Sonia, maybe you should explain it."

Sonia did her best. "I was thinking that, you know how some people believe there are alternate universes? Where stuff that almost happened but didn't in our universe did happen?"

Vincent and I nodded politely.

"Sure," said Steve.

"Well, what if the cafeteria is some sort of point of connection between our universe and another one, and—"

"And what we're seeing is a small tear in the fabric of space-time between the two that occurs at midnight?" Steve interrupted.

"Yes!" said Sonia. "See?" she said to Laura and Hoppy. "Steve knows what I'm talking about."

Steve doesn't even know what Steve's *talking about*, I thought but didn't say.

Hoppy concluded: "So we decided we'd check it out."

"Us too!" said Steve. "But how did you get in?"

"I went to the office for a bus pass this afternoon," said Sonia. "There was no one out front, and there were all those shiny keys dangling there. . . ."

"Right?" said Steve.

Sonia made an I'm-so-bad face and confessed: "So I lifted one of the keys to the loading dock by the kitchen. And I decided to test out my theory. With some help, of course." She nodded at her henchwomen.

"Brilliant," said Steve.

Sonia rolled her eyes modestly and beamed.

"It's almost time," said Hoppy. "We should go back in the cafeteria. We only came out here to see what the noise was."

"We weren't making any noise," said Vincent.

"Then what was that crashing sound?" said Hoppy.

"We didn't make a crashing sound," I said.

"It sounded like someone knocked over a trash can."

"It wasn't us."

"Huh," said Hoppy. "Oh well. We better get inside if we want to see anything."

"Wait a minute," I said. On the one hand, I thought Steve and Sonia's theory of a tear in space-time was ridiculous. On the other hand, what if you could get sucked in?

"Why?" said Hoppy and Steve together.

"Well," I hedged, "maybe we should wait *outside* the cafeteria. Watch what happens from here. So we don't, um,

71

interfere with the space-time continuum or whatever."

"He has a point," said Sonia.

"He has no idea what he's talking about," said Vincent.

"Neither do y—"

"It makes sense," said Laura.

She spoke so rarely that we stopped bickering and looked at her.

Laura went red under the glare of our attention. Then she said, "We don't want to interfere with whatever is going to happen, do we?"

"No, we don't," said Steve. "We can watch from outside the doors. We'll prop them open—that isn't interfering, is it?" he asked Laura.

I don't know why he'd decided that Laura was the expert on interference, when I was the one who'd brought it up originally.

Laura didn't seem to know either. She just peered at Steve from behind her hair.

Sonia and Vincent propped the doors open.

As the dimly lit clock in the cafeteria ticked toward midnight, the six of us assembled like a studio audience right outside the doorway. I carefully positioned myself behind Steve and Sonia. Who knew what kind of alternate-universe energy waves might come splashing out at us when midnight arrived?

chapter
18

"IT'S MIDNIGHT," HOPPY SAID NEEDLESSLY.

I could feel Vincent's hot breath on the side of my neck as he leaned to see into the cafeteria. It was kind of comforting, to be honest.

"Is anything happening?" I asked, since I couldn't really see past Steve and Sonia.

"Nope," said Steve. "Nothing."

My armpits were starting to prickle with emerging sweat.

"How long do we wait?" Sonia asked.

"It always happens right at midnight on the recording," said Hoppy. "It's three past now."

"Maybe the clock is fast," said Vincent.

"Maybe."

We waited some more. Then Steve said, "I think I

saw something move. In the cafeteria. Over by the drink machine. See?"

Vincent shoved me aside and I let him.

"It's people!" Sonia whispered. She paused. "But why is it still dark in there? Shouldn't the lights be on?"

"It's Nikhil," said Hoppy. "And Andrew."

"Where's everybody else?" said Sonia.

"Wait," said Steve. "Are they coming over here? They shouldn't be able to see us, should they?"

"Why not?" said Sonia. "We can see them."

"But we're not part of their universe," said Steve.

"And they're not part of ours," Sonia replied. "It makes sense."

Whatever she meant, it didn't.

The whole group was now moving backward, away from the doorway and the alternate Nikhil and Andrew. I can't speak for the rest, but I was gearing up to run for my ever-loving life.

"Guys!" said the other Nikhil. "What are you doing here? You're interfering. No wonder nothing happened."

Nikhil stood in the cafeteria doorway, frowning at us with his mustache-less face. Andrew came up beside him, normal (for him) size, un-muscular, and clearly annoyed.

"You're you," said Steve.

"Of course we're us."

"We thought you might be—"

"The alternate us from another dimension?" said Andrew.

"Yeah."

"No. Sorry."

The entire H.A.I.R. Club spent some time getting used to the idea that we'd all showed up at school at midnight expecting something to happen that wasn't going to.

"How did you two get in?" Hoppy said finally.

"Well, we were thinking we'd jimmy a window," said Nikhil. "But—"

"Jimmy a window?" said Hoppy. "Are you kidding? Do you even know what jimmying is?"

"Not really," said Andrew. "We were planning to improvise."

"What, exactly," Hoppy pressed, "were you going to jimmy a window with?"

"I don't know," said Nikhil. "Some type of jimmier?"

Hoppy let out a breath so forcefully some stray curls blew off her forehead, but she didn't say anything. She admitted to me later that she had no idea what jimmying involved either.

"Anyway," said Nikhil, "we didn't have to do any jimmying, because someone left the door to the loading dock by the kitchen open."

"Oops," said Sonia.

"So we strolled right in."

"At least that explains the noise a while ago," said Hoppy. "Did you knock over a trash can or something?"

"No," said Andrew. "We were totally silent. Weren't we?" he asked Nikhil.

Nikhil nodded. "Like ninjas," he said.

"Huh," said Hoppy.

"I guess we should go," I ventured when no one else had said anything for a moment. "Looks like the whole alternate-universe thing is a bust."

"We'll have to modify the A.U. theory, at least," said Andrew. "Now that we have some data."

"You guys interfered," said Nikhil. "You interfered with the A.U. theory data."

"You two were the ones inside the cafeteria," said Steve. "If anyone interfered with the whatever data, it was you."

"Um," said Andrew, "can we save this argument for later?"

"Why?" said Vincent. "It's already later. We might as well—"

"Because if we don't get away from here now, we are going to be interfered *with*," said Andrew.

He pointed down the hallway.

Sure enough, the one character still missing from the scene was making its entrance: The crouton-loving skunk was trotting toward us like a friendly dog expecting a treat.

chapter
19

"EVERYONE STAY STILL," SAID HOPPY. "AND BE QUIET. Maybe it will keep going by us."

We stood still, but the quiet part was more challenging.

"We're standing in the cafeteria doorway," Andrew whispered. "Doesn't that put us between it and its croutons?"

"Crud," said Steve. Because the skunk was still heading right for us.

"Okay, everybody shuffle sideways. *Slowly!*" said Hoppy. "Give it some room."

We group-shuffled to make way for the skunk to enter the cafeteria. We were past the doorway now, leaving it free and clear.

The skunk regarded the wide-open passage, then sat down. And turned its attention to us.

Since I'd been at the back of the group looking into the cafeteria, I was now at the front of the group being looked at by the skunk. I tried to smile in a reassuring "we mean you no harm" way at it—without showing my teeth, which I knew from reading something somewhere was a bad thing to do with animals. Though maybe that was just dogs.

"Let's back away slowly down the hall," I said as clearly as possible while smiling idiotically and not showing my teeth.

We shuffled backward. I kept my frozen smile aimed at the skunk. We were almost to the door to the girls' locker room and safety when the skunk got up and started following us.

"Do we look like croutons?" said Vincent.

Apparently we did. We backed right up to the locker room door. Sonia, who was nearest, pushed the door open and we all basically fell inside.

"Shut the door!" Hoppy hissed.

I obeyed.

"What's it doing?" asked Steve.

I peered through the long, narrow window in the locker room door.

"Sitting right outside," I said. "Grooming or something."

It was dark in the girls' locker room, and smellier than I would have guessed. A lot less smelly than the boys' locker room, but still. I would have thought that the girls' locker room smelled like perfume, or at least deodorant. Not so.

The girls guided us through a maze of lockers and shower stalls to the door that led to the gym. We emerged into the gym, and I took a deep breath of air that was better than the locker room's but still had a ways to go toward genuine freshness.

"Let's get out of here," said Hoppy.

We were halfway across the gym when Andrew, who seemed to have some kind of skunk-radar, said, "Don't look now, but our new B.F. is headed this way."

Sure enough, the skunk was trotting eagerly toward us, nails clicking on the gym floor.

"Does that thing teleport?" Vincent asked.

"Maybe it came through the boys' locker room," said Nikhil.

I wondered if even a skunk would mind the smell in there. Probably.

"Okay," said Steve. "Don't panic. We'll just keep moving calmly toward the exit."

But as soon as we moved, the skunk darted at us.

"Okay," said Steve again. "We're going to have to wait it out."

So there we were, the entire membership of the Flounder Bay Upper School H.A.I.R. Club, somehow trapped in the gym by one skunk.

Eventually, tired and stiff from standing there, we started sinking one by one to the floor. The skunk sat down too, but it didn't take its eyes off us.

"Maybe it's lonely," said Sonia when the standoff (now sit-off) had gone on for fifteen minutes.

"Then it should find some skunk friends. Outside. Where skunks live," Andrew grumbled.

"I have a math test tomorrow," said Nikhil. "And Jason, if you don't stop humming, I'm going to grab that skunk and aim it at you."

"We all have to be home before our parents wake up," I said. "Or the janitors come in. What time do the janitors come in?"

No one knew.

"When do skunks go to bed?" Vincent asked.

"I think they're nocturnal," said Hoppy. "Sunrise?"

"Maybe if we act really boring, it will get tired of us and leave," said Steve.

"I don't see how we can act more boring than we are now," said Nikhil.

He was right, but the skunk seemed more interested in us than ever. It got up and wandered over to our group. Our group responded by clustering together until things got pretty uncomfortable. The skunk ignored our discomfort. It walked right up to me and—to my horror—nudged its head under my elbow.

"Help!" I said in the tiniest whisper I could.

"Nobody move," said Hoppy, even as she and the others started inching away from me.

"What does it *want*?" Vincent managed to whisper hysterically.

"It's behaving like a cat," Steve said. "Like it wants to be petted."

"It *is* lonely," said Sonia. "Poor thing."

"Well?" said Steve to me.

"Well, what?"

"Pet it!"

"Are you kidding?"

"Pretend it's a cat," said Hoppy.

"Why don't *you* pet it?"

"It *chose you.*"

Curse my friendly smile!

I closed my eyes and pretended that the skunk was a cat. I reached out and petted it, very gently, from head to tail. And it seemed okay with that. So I did it again. And again. I petted a skunk while my friends and colleagues continued to inch away from me toward the door to the outside.

This wasn't exactly throwing myself on a grenade or anything, but it was some level of heroic, I think. And I wasn't going to let them forget it. Ever.

chapter 20

IN THE END, THE SKUNK HELD THE H.A.I.R. CLUB
hostage until 2:15 a.m., when it simply trotted off, probably in search of tasty croutons. Vincent and I were back
in bed by three. And four hours later, the alarm went off.

None of us was looking good that day at school. We'd
see each other in the hallway and nod weakly at our fellow
zombie, then shamble off to our next class. It seemed as if
our ordeal had bonded us, which felt good. Especially since
I (at least) considered myself the hero of the night. But by
the time we had assembled in H.A.I.R. headquarters that
afternoon, we were way past bonded and well into irritable.

Nikhil had taken one of the two chairs and was resting his head on the desk in front of it. When everyone
was there, he managed to lift his head. "I'm going to play
the recording for last night," he said. "Even though I'm

pretty sure there won't be anything on it, since you guys interfered."

"We did not interfere," said Steve. "We weren't in the cafeteria at midnight. If anything, it was you two—"

He stopped because Nikhil had already gotten to midnight on last night's recording, and instead of Nikhil, Andrew, and possibly a skunk in the dark cafeteria, there was the usual crowd of not-quite-us, having lunch in broad daylight.

"What the what?" said Vincent. "That did *not* happen last night."

"So it can't be an A.U. thing," said Sonia. "Unless it's an invisible alternate universe?"

"An I.A.U.," said Andrew quietly.

"If it's invisible, how does it appear on the camera?" asked Hoppy.

"It's not a normal camera," Steve said.

I was only half paying attention to this discussion, since I was busy trying to find myself among the kids in the cafeteria.

"Maybe . . . ," said Andrew slowly. "Maybe this is a prank."

"What do you mean?" asked Hoppy.

"I mean, what if the security system took the pictures it has of us and . . ." Andrew paused to collect his thoughts.

No one said anything.

"And pasted them onto the bodies of other people who were in the cafeteria at noon," Andrew concluded.

"Right!" said Hoppy. "I mean, that definitely isn't my body. Though it does look like my mother's. And she wasn't in the cafeteria at noon."

"But did the security system paste a mustache on me?" Nikhil asked.

"It could have," said Andrew. "It could have borrowed a mustache from someone else."

"Couldn't it have borrowed a better one?" I muttered.

"That totally explains my hair," said Steve over my muttering. "That *has* to be the explanation. That is *borrowed* hair."

"But," said Vincent.

"But what?" said Steve.

"But why? Why would a security system prank us? It's not clever and it's not funny. It's not mean. It's got none of the essential qualities of a successful prank."

"It did have us going, though," said Steve. "I mean, alternate universes? Come on."

"That was your theory!"

"Not anymore. My hair couldn't look like that even in an alternate universe."

No one knew quite what to say. It had been such a cool mystery—and now it boiled down to an unsuccessful prank by an anonymous security system? If that was the solution, it was disappointing.

We let the recording play for a while.

We saw Hoppy. She was speaking earnestly with the woman working the cafeteria cash register. She was pointing. We watched the woman reorganize the bills in the cash drawer as Hoppy nodded approvingly.

We saw Sonia. She was wearing a faded denim jacket with patches sewn all over it. She was showing the boy she was with (not the pirate-blouse-makeup boy) how to sew a patch on his matching denim jacket.

"Wait, though," said Nikhil.

Which was weird, since none of us was exactly rushing to do anything at this point.

"Here's the thing," Nikhil added.

"Yes?" Hoppy prompted.

Nikhil wasn't usually one for hesitation, and—was that embarrassment on his face? It might have been. I had never seen Nikhil embarrassed. That was more of a Jason thing.

"I was thinking about growing a mustache," Nikhil said. "Planning to, actually. When I could, I mean. What?" he asked when he saw the collective expression on our faces. "I had no idea it would be that awful. My dad has a mustache and his looks good."

"That's true," said Steve. "But his doesn't look like something that barely survived a harsh winter collapsed on his upper lip."

"Okay, okay," said Nikhil. "The point is—"

"Yes, what is the point here?" I said. "I mean, what does it matter if you were planning to grow a mustache?"

"It matters because how could a security system know that?" said Nikhil. "Why would it choose me for a mustache? Why not Steve?"

"No way!" said Steve. "I would never grow a mustache."

"That's what I mean," said Nikhil. "It can't read minds, so how did I end up with a mustache?"

"I recently bought a bowling shirt," said Sonia.

This conversation was zigging and zagging around so much I was getting a headache.

"A bowling shirt? Why?" asked Hoppy. "Unless you bowl. Do you bowl?"

"I've never bowled," said Sonia. "I was at a thrift store, and I found this bowling shirt that had 'Sonia' embroidered on it. I had to buy it, right?"

"Of course you did," said Steve.

"That's what I thought. But what if it wasn't a one-off bowling shirt?" Sonia asked. "What if it was a gateway purchase? What if it's the beginning of my descent into weird fashion choices and matching boyfriends?"

"A bowling shirt does leave the door wide open for pirate blouses," said Hoppy. "And whatever statement those denim jackets are trying too hard to make."

"Um," said Laura from behind the other laptop. "I started guitar lessons over the summer."

There was a baffled pause until she zoomed the big-screen picture in on a poster on the cafeteria wall. The poster said FALL DANCE FEATURING FBUS'S HOTTEST BAND, LARA AND THE LARIATS! TICKETS ON SALE FRIDAY. We couldn't make out any of the smaller type below that.

"Oh my gosh," said Sonia. "That is such a cool band name."

"What on earth," I said slowly, losing all patience with the irrelevant zigs and zags, "does some girl named Lara's band have to do with Laura taking guitar lessons?"

I assumed the silence that followed was admiration for my logic. But it turned out not to be that. It turned out to be horror at my chuckleheadedness.

"Dude," said Vincent finally. "Her name is Lara. Not Laura."

chapter
21

LAURA ANDERSEN'S NAME WAS LARA ANDERSEN. IT always had been, and everyone knew that except me. I tried to calculate how many times I had called her Laura, and at first I was relieved to think that I had never called her by any name. Which is why no one had corrected me until now.

The fact was that Laura/Lara Andersen was of so little interest to me that I had never talked about her. I had relegated her to a two-dimensional minor-character role in my life to the extent that she was just Shy Girl from Math Class and H.A.I.R. Club and nothing more.

This could have been my low point. I could have recognized my mistake and apologized to Lara and vowed to pay better attention to the people around me and lived up to that vow. But it was not my low point. I had still lower points to achieve. And one of them occurred immediately after the Laura/Lara revelation.

Here's what I said: "Laura, Lara, whatever."

Yes, I was tired and cranky and my head ached. And yes, I was embarrassed and wanted to move on. But still . . . My parents hadn't brought me up to be such a chucklehead.

"So what if the program knows that one of us wants to grow a mustache or play guitar?" I went on, trying to guide the conversation back to the actual topic. "Maybe it's a good guesser. Or maybe it somehow reads our Internet stuff."

"I did *not* announce my plans to grow a mustache on the Internet," said Nikhil. "That's private."

"Plus, it made a big mistake with me," said Andrew. "Zoom in on me," he said to Nikhil. "Right next to where you and Steve are."

Nikhil brought the image up on the big screen.

"See?" said Andrew. "That's me. But I'm wearing an MIT sweatshirt. Not my UC Santa Barbara sweatshirt."

"At least this one fits you," said Vincent.

"But it's wrong," said Andrew. "I have absolutely no plans to apply to MIT. And I would only wear a sweatshirt from someplace I wanted to go."

"That's kind of eccentric," said Hoppy.

"Why wouldn't you want to go to MIT?" Steve asked, reasonably enough.

"No surfing," said Andrew.

"You *surf*?" said Steve.

"Yes, I do," said Andrew. "Why? Is there something you think I might be better at? Something to do with spherical orange objects being thrown through hoops?"

"Um," said Steve. "No, not at all. I mean, the water in Flounder Bay is so cold."

"Uh-huh," said Andrew. "And while we're on the topic of my extracurriculars, I play clarinet. Not piano."

Steve just looked baffled at this.

"Guys," said Hoppy. "Stop talking for a sec. Move the focus to the left," she told Nikhil. "By your elbow."

"Like this, Your Majesty?"

"Yes. Now zoom in as close as you can on the newspaper."

"It's just the *Flyer*," said Vincent.

The *FBUS Flyer* was the school paper. Most kids used it to mop up spills—it was more absorbent than the water-repellent napkins the cafeteria stocked.

Sure enough, the paper by Andrew's elbow was blotted with ketchup.

"Can anyone read the date on the paper?" said Hoppy.

No one could. The focus was too fuzzy. But we could make out the headline:

PRINCIPAL WU ANNOUNCES NEW MENU

FOR CAFETERIA

"That's a relief," said Vincent. "The old menu is— Wait. Principal Wu? Wu is the vice principal."

"Yes, she is," said Hoppy.

"In this universe, anyway," said Sonia.

"Can you try one more thing?" Hoppy asked Nikhil.

"Aye, aye, Captain."

"See if there's a calendar on the wall."

Nikhil switched views to the wall where the big calendar hung in the cafeteria as we knew it. And there it was.

"That might be easier to read," said Hoppy.

She was right. Everyone could see the month and year printed across the top.

"That's five years from now," said Vincent.

chapter
22

ALL THE MEMBERS OF THE FLOUNDER BAY H.A.I.R.
Club except Hoppy were staring at Hoppy.

"What?" she said.

"How did you know?" said Sonia.

"Know what?"

"About the calendar."

"It's the only thing that makes sense," said Hoppy. "A security system isn't going to play pranks on us or look at our Internet posts. Or read our minds."

"And what makes more sense to you," said Nikhil carefully, "is that a security system is somehow showing us the future?"

Hoppy shrugged. "It was just a guess."

"You read too much science fiction," said Vincent.

"I don't read any science fiction," said Hoppy.

"I bet you've read *A Wrinkle in Time*," I said.

"Okay, yes," said Hoppy. "But not time-travel stuff."

"Technically," I said, "*A Wrinkle in Time* does involve time tr—"

"Can we focus, please?" said Steve. "We're almost out of time."

"Focus on what?" I asked.

"On the fact," said Steve, "that the futuristic calendar and newspaper could be part of the prank. Right?"

"Oh no," said Vincent. "Now we're back to the stupid prank theory when things were starting to be cool again?"

"You're just worried that your hair really will look like that in five years," Hoppy said to Steve.

"Not at all," said Steve. "I just think a prank is way more reasonable as an explanation than some sort of time-traveling security camera."

"The camera itself wouldn't necessarily have to travel in time," said Andrew. "The security files could travel somehow . . . which might explain why the midnight files aren't as clear and easy to navigate as the others. They weren't recorded on this system. It's theoretically kind of interesting. . . ."

"Not to mention impossible," said Steve.

But he was losing the crowd. The rest of us were way more intrigued by the idea of files from the future than we were by some program randomly pranking us.

"Um," said Lara. "One thing that makes sense? About the future idea?"

"Yes?" said Hoppy, as Steve opened his mouth to object.

"The name of the company," said Lara. "Prescient Technologies."

"What about it?" said Vincent. "Company names don't mean anything."

"True," said Nikhil. "Woozle? That's not even a word."

"It is too," I said. "It's from *Winnie-the-Pooh*."

"It's not a real word," said Nikhil.

"So 'prescient' is a real word?" said Vincent.

"Yeah. It means something like being able to see the future," said Andrew. "Right?" He turned to Lara.

She nodded.

"That hair is *not* my future," said Steve. "And besides, we have to finish up. Nikhil and I have a cross-country meeting this afternoon."

"And I have Haiku Club after this," said Vincent.

As we headed upstairs, a disturbing thought sprouted like a poisonous mushroom in my mind. I still hadn't seen myself in any of the midnight recordings. So if they did show the future, there was something wrong with mine. Specifically, I wasn't in it. My stomach clenched and I forgot to take a breath for a few seconds as this sank in.

"Steve," I said when we'd arrived on the first floor. "Can I borrow the key for a little while? I want to go back and . . . ah, check on something. I'll drop it off in half an hour."

"Okay," he said.

"Thanks." I took the key and hurried back down to the basement.

My hand was shaking as I put the key in the lock. My other hand was shaking as I flipped on the light. Both hands shook together as I logged on to a laptop and brought up last night's recording again.

What if I searched the whole cafeteria and still couldn't find myself? If Hoppy was right and this was the future and I wasn't in it, what did that mean?

chapter
23

CALM DOWN, I TOLD MYSELF. BREATHE. JUST BECAUSE *you're not in one particular room five years from now doesn't mean you don't* exist *five years from now. And that's what you're worried about, right? Existing?*

And yes, existing was my main concern. But not my only one. What if I had been in a terrible accident and was so disfigured that I didn't recognize myself? What if I had committed a crime and was in some sort of juvenile-detention facility? What if the bookstore had gone out of business and my family had moved away from Flounder Bay?

I decided that lurching around the cafeteria in terror and zooming in on every kid who remotely resembled me wasn't the best use of my limited time. I needed to use a grid system, the way they search for missing hikers in the wilderness. But trying to impose a neat grid on the chaos of a school cafeteria is not as easy as it sounds. Especially since I had to keep right-clicking to change views. I was starting to feel sweaty and nauseated when the door to the janitors' closet opened.

I nearly fell out of the chair.

"Sorry," said Lara as she crept around the door into the room. "I didn't mean to startle you. I left my gym bag in here."

"I'm not startled," I said.

"Are you okay?" she asked. "You look kind of—"

"Of course I'm okay, why wouldn't I be okay?" I had no control at all over the pitch of my voice.

She picked up her bag, which was behind my chair.

"Are you looking for yourself?" she asked.

Now she was chatty? The girl who wouldn't eke out a "help" if her hair was on fire was all willing to make small talk now that I was mid-crisis?

She did seem less shy than usual, I couldn't help noticing. She was standing behind me with her bag over her shoulder and a hand on a hip: not her usual stooped "don't notice me" posture. Maybe it was because I was sitting and she was standing, but she seemed taller.

"No, I'm not looking for myself," I said, as if that were the stupidest thing I could possibly have been doing.

"You're right there," said Lara, jabbing a forefinger at the screen. "Across from Vincent."

"That isn't me," I objected after a millisecond of

checking out the back of the kid sitting with Vincent. "What makes you think that's me?"

Lara didn't answer. She was already out the door.

I zoomed in on the table. Vincent was surrounded by textbooks, and he was scribbling in a notebook, an elbow in his abandoned lunch.

The only other person at the table was the boy across from him. He had his back to the camera, but it was obvious that he was a big kid with a thick neck to match.

We need to pause for a minute, because here's something you should know about me before we continue. As I've said, I was spectacularly ordinary in seventh grade. The one thing that set me apart was my neck. My scrawny little neck. Picture that baby bird from the picture book *Are You My Mother?*, then subtract the beak and add a pointy Adam's apple. That was me. So this kid with the sturdy neck couldn't be me.

His hair color was the same as mine, but medium brown is a common hair color. His black sweatshirt was something I would wear, but it was also something almost everyone at Flounder Bay Upper School would wear. There was something familiar about him, though, even from the back.

Then his head turned partway, and I realized what made me think that. He reminded me of my uncle Luke. He looked like Luke would if he were in high school. And that's easy to imagine because Luke still kind of looks like he's in high school.

I changed the view so I could see all of the kid's face: his face, Uncle Luke's face, and also, I realized, my face.

I'd never realized how much of the way I thought I looked was based on my trademark scrawny neck. And the matching scrawny body underneath it. I didn't know what to think now, confronted by this larger me.

And as I wondered about this, it occurred to me that I believed Hoppy's theory. This had to be the future me. There was no way a computer program could have taken the baby-bird-necked picture of me from a couple of weeks ago and mutated it into the Luke-ish kid on the screen.

I let the action move forward for a while, studying my future self as he ate his lunch and talked (with his mouth full) to Vincent, who didn't respond or even look up.

Vincent was older and bigger too, but his transformation was nothing like mine. Physically, anyway. Behaviorally was a different story. Seventh-grade Vincent wasn't one to do homework during lunch. Or to look like he hadn't slept for the past week. Future Vincent appeared to need a long rest and some vitamins.

Future Jason finished his lunch and sat back in his chair. I studied him, trying to assess him as if he were a stranger, the way you sometimes try to catch yourself in a shop window and see how you look to others. Was he good-looking? Did he seem happy? But it was too late. Now that I recognized myself, I could no longer be impartial. He was already too familiar to judge.

Then, as I watched, future Jason sat up straight. His

attention was riveted by something off camera, over Vincent's shoulder. His hand went up to his hair in an embarrassingly self-conscious gesture that I recognized as one of my own. I decided never to do it again. A dopey grin developed on his face. It was almost enough to make me decide never to smile again. Now his gaze was tracking from right to left. He looked like a cat watching a bird outside a window.

Vincent glanced up from his work and said something to Jason. Jason's grin disappeared as he responded— rudely, I was pretty sure. Then he went back to staring at whatever it was he was staring at. I switched views so I could see what he was seeing.

Then I did. It was a girl.

chapter 24

THE GIRL WAS VISIBLE BRIEFLY AND ONLY FROM THE side, as she slipped through the cafeteria doorway. She was tall and—what's the word I'm looking for? Ms. Grossman would know. Willowy? Something like that. She had short blond hair that came to two points at her chin. She was dressed in black. She was gone.

I followed her into the hall, where suddenly everything went dark.

I wiggled the cursor around uselessly, which is what I always do when a computer disappoints me. Then I saw something wander across the screen. My old friend the skunk. It seemed that once you left the cafeteria, you were in the present.

I moved back into the cafeteria, hoping to see more of the girl who had attracted future Jason's attention. But the stupid door to the janitors' closet banged open again.

"You said half an hour," said Steve.

"Sorry. I'm almost done. I need—"

"You *are* done. They're about to close the office. Come on."

I shut the laptop down and locked the door behind us. Then I handed the key to Steve.

He took it without a word, and we walked up the stairs. When we reached the main hallway, Steve turned to me.

"Did you find yourself?" he asked.

"Yeah," I said.

"Good," he said. "I was starting to worry that you'd moved away or something. In the future, I mean."

"Nope," I said. "In fact, there's more of me than ever."

By the time I got home I was almost falling over from lack of sleep and also from the weird turns the day had taken. I barely managed to stagger into the house.

"You're late," said Alice. She was wearing a paper crown and stood in the middle of the hallway, blocking my path, like the opposite of the Statue of Liberty.

"For what?"

"For rehearsals. You have to be in my show tonight. It needs two people."

"There's no way I'm going to be in your show tonight or any night."

"I'm telling Mom."

"Be my guest."

"Mooooooooooom!"

I didn't wait for Mom's response. I went upstairs to my room and flopped onto my bed with my sneakers and backpack still on. It was extremely uncomfortable. I remained there anyway.

I kept picturing the expression on future me's face as he watched that girl in the cafeteria. Why was he so interested in her?

Maybe she was new and he was curious about her. Possible, but that intense stare seemed to be about more than idle curiosity. Maybe she had stolen something from him. But if so, why just stare at her? Why not go up to her and demand it back? Maybe he suspected that she'd stolen something but wasn't sure and was trying to figure out if she had it by staring at her. That one was so pathetic I almost convinced myself it was the answer. This was me we were dealing with, after all.

But in the end, as the dinner smells started wafting upstairs and I finally removed my backpack before it fused with my spine, I admitted the truth to myself. Future me had a crush on that girl in black. A major crush.

"Jason! Dinner!" my dad called.

Grateful for the distraction, I went downstairs.

Where, after dinner, my mom proceeded to browbeat me into "helping your little sister" with her ridiculous "performance."

Alice's two-person show was called *Dork, Dork, Goose*. Her role was to walk in circles around me, slapping my head and saying, "Dork, dork, dork, dork . . ." over and over again. The longer it went on, the harder the slaps got. My role was to sit there and be slapped. I, and possibly my parents, figured that eventually she'd say "Goose!" and start to run. At which point I intended to let her keep running and hope she didn't come back.

Instead, what she didn't do was say "Goose!" The show ended when she got so dizzy from walking in circles that she fell over. My dad had to carry her upstairs to her room.

My mother actually clapped as Alice was borne away. "It was like *Waiting for Godot*," she said to me. "You keep expecting something to happen, and the point is that it doesn't. It's really very intriguing."

"It was really an excuse to hit me and call me a dork."

"You're very patient with her, and I appreciate that," said my mother.

I was so tired by now that I kind of wanted my dad to carry me up to bed. But I was way too old and dignified for that.

chapter
25

THE NEXT MEETING OF THE H.A.I.R. CLUB DIDN'T GO
as expected. We were just getting settled when Ms. Grossman knocked on the door by shouting, "Knock, knock!"
and then let herself in, followed by a guy in a park-ranger
or big-game-hunter costume of some kind, lots of khaki
and utility pockets.

"H.A.I.R. Club," said Ms. Grossman, "this is Neil
Drumlin, from the Flounder Bay Natural History Museum.
You've all been there, right?"

We nodded. Of course we'd been there. The museum
had nature trails and woodland exhibits and farm animals,
and also some wild animals that had been injured and
couldn't live in the wild anymore.

"Neil's here to take a look at the skunk recordings,"
said Ms. Grossman. "Steve told me that's what's been

cadging the cafeteria croutons." She chuckled a bit at this. "Sorry—couldn't resist," she added, not sorry at all.

"Hey, everyone," said Neil in a practiced-at-talking-to-kids voice. "Ms. Grossman called to ask me about removing the skunk, but I'm hoping we can do better than that."

What could have been better than removing it? I wondered. Officially enrolling it at the school? Getting the cafeteria's crouton recipe for it?

"The thing is," Neil continued, "I'm hoping that your skunk is actually *my* skunk. One of our resident skunks, Penelope, wandered off a couple of weeks ago when we were cleaning her enclosure. She may have come over here and gotten hooked on your croutons—she does love her carbs. And she also loves people—she's completely tame and de-scented. She used to be someone's pet, believe it or not. Never do that," he added quickly. "Wild animals aren't pets, and also it's illegal."

This explained a lot, if you'll recall my encounter with the skunk. I was sort of sorry now that I hadn't been friendlier to it. Because sure enough, as soon as Steve had found a bit of skunk recording and zoomed in on its face, Neil let out a shout of recognition.

"That's my girl," he said happily.

Don't ask me what he saw there that he recognized. It looked like a generic skunk face to me.

"I have to set a few traps," Neil said. "Bait them with some peanut-butter crackers. Those are her favorites."

"Traps?" said Sonia. "That's so cruel! You can't use traps!"

"Not to worry," said Neil. "Humane traps. She goes in, she has a snack, and she can't get out till I let her out. She'll be safe and sound. But thanks for your concern."

"Mystery solved, then," said Ms. Grossman. "Thanks, H.A.I.R. Club!"

"Hey," said Neil, "if any of you want to help set the traps, I'll make some extra peanut-butter crackers for you."

I shook my head. Poor Neil. He actually thought a few salty snacks could convince us to schlep around the school setting skunk traps. Little did he know that we had our futures to discover instead.

Actually, little did I know the attraction of peanut-butter crackers in the late afternoon. Especially for kids who ate lunch at ten thirty. Everyone except me volunteered immediately.

"Great!" said Ms. Grossman. She saw me settling into a chair and said, "Lock up, will you, Jason?"

I nodded.

Steve raised his eyebrows questioningly. Then he tossed me the key, and everyone filed out, leaving me alone.

I brought up the recording from last night and focused on the table that Vincent and I had been sitting at the day before. Sure enough, there we were.

Future me was eating like utensils and napkins were unknown to him. Poor future Vincent was probably being sprayed by wet food bits as future Jason blathered away at him, but he clearly didn't have the energy to protect himself.

Vincent and future me were alone at the table, as we had been before. And as I watched us sitting there without Steve or any of the other people Steve tended to attract, I felt my stomach lurch the way it does if you bend over while you're riding in an elevator. I felt sick, and it wasn't from watching myself eat.

I realized that what I was feeling was pity. I pitied my future self, who seemed to be down to one friend. A friend who was probably just too tired to get up and find better company. And then I felt a cold little stab of fear in my already queasy stomach.

If that was my future, I really didn't like the look of it.

I was about to stop the recording, when lunch period ended onscreen. As most kids left for class, future me started doing something I recognized as stalling. He gathered his trash and started piling it slowly and neatly on his tray. He folded his unused napkin, unfolded it, refolded it, and set it delicately atop the rest. For me, neatness is almost always about stalling.

Finally, Vincent left him alone with his fussy trash stack. Future me got up immediately, heaved the carefully arranged tray into the trash, and glanced around. He was up to something he wasn't proud of. But what?

chapter 26

HERE'S WHERE THE STORY GETS EVEN MORE PER-sonally embarrassing for me. You're thinking that I look pretty bad already—what more could possibly be coming? A lot, unfortunately. But I'm a historian, and my objective is to tell the truth, no matter who gets humiliated along the way. So far it's been mainly me, and going forward it will still be mainly me. But that's the price I pay for truth-telling.

Future me waited until almost everyone was out of the cafeteria. A few kids I didn't recognize lingered by the trash cans, but I guess they didn't matter, because now he made his move. He rushed over to the wall with the calendar on it, reached up, and expertly—as if he'd done this before so many times he'd gotten good at it—took down a poster for the upcoming dance featuring Lara and the Lariats.

Weird, huh? Did he not want anyone to go to the dance? If so, he was too late—the poster had been up for days. Was he planning to deface the poster? If so, why not deface it while it was still on the wall, like a normal vandal? He seemed to have planned this in advance—he could have brought a Sharpie.

But no. He didn't write on it or tear it up or throw it away. He didn't even fold it. He carefully rolled it up, then he pulled an elastic band out of his pocket (he *had* come prepared!) and slipped it around the tube. Which he gently slid into his backpack.

Then he walked jauntily out of the cafeteria, a smug smile on his face.

I may not be as good at math as some, but I can add two and two and get four. So it took mere moments for me to add yesterday's crush on a mysterious blond girl and today's poster-stealing and come up with the blaringly obvious: Future me had a crush on a mysterious blond girl who was in Lara's band. Lara was blond. Lara was in her band. Therefore . . . I can't bring myself to write it. You can do it in the space provided here:

Future Jason had a huge and embarrassing
crush on future _____.

There. You wrote it. Happy?
I wasn't. And here's more about why.
Lara Andersen hated me. *Hated* me. Ever since I had

revealed that I didn't know her name and didn't care that I didn't know it, Lara's attitude toward me had changed. Before, she had just acted shy. In math class, in the halls, at club meetings—she'd see me coming and duck her head; she'd look away if I sat near her; she'd answer in a whisper if I asked her a question. But at least it was a friendly whisper.

Now she seemed more sure of herself around me. Sure of her intense dislike for me. As an example: This morning I had come to the end of my pencil eraser's usefulness in math. So I asked Lara if I could borrow a pencil. She looked directly at me, all right, and it was not a look people normally give other humans. It was more the kind of look people give something from way back in their refrigerator and way, way back in time. Then she grabbed a pencil from her case and flipped it onto my desk without comment. The kicker? It didn't have any eraser left on it.

So if future Lara felt about future Jason anything like present Lara felt about present Jason (and it appeared that she did, or why was he reduced to stealing posters?), then . . . future Jason was out of luck.

My current problem was that Lara herself was fully capable of adding two and two and getting four. In fact, she was better at math than I was, as our performance in class showed. Which meant that if she saw the recording I'd just seen, she was going to know that the kid she hated was going to have a huge, sloppy, hopeless crush on her in five years. And it was possible, I had to admit to myself with horror, that she might assume that the kid she hated had a huge, sloppy, hopeless crush on her now. I couldn't live with that. I just could not.

My future self, with his one remaining friend and one-sided, obsessive crush, did *not* need Lara feeling sorry for him on top of his other issues. And my present self didn't need her feeling stalked by one or both of us. Her hostility was bad enough.

It was obvious what I needed to do. I needed to erase this recording, or at least the end of it. There had to be a delete function, right?

I brought up the home screen and searched for anything like a delete command. Nothing. Then I brought up the recording itself, minimized it a bit, and searched that screen for a nice big X. Or a trash can icon—those were always handy. Nothing.

All right. I hated to do it, it went against everything I stood for, but I was desperate. I looked around for a help symbol. Which I found where all help symbols live: in the upper-right corner of the screen. A nice red question mark. I clicked on it.

A box popped open. It read:

Tailored-Wording Enriched Response Program (T.W.E.R.P.) engaged.

Hello, Jason. What do you want to know?

This was weirdly casual, but okay.

How do I delete a recording? I typed.

Recordings are automatically deleted after ten years with no views.

What if I want to delete one sooner than that? I asked.

Recordings can be deleted prior to ten years by an Authorized User.

Who is an Authorized User? I asked.

The current Authorized User for this system is: Yvonne Wu.

Great. Only the vice principal could delete my embarrassing file. I tried one more angle.

Can I delete part of a recording? I typed.

Partial recordings can be deleted by an Authorized User.

Great again. But it wasn't quite done. Another line appeared below:

The exception is +5 files, which are auto-deleted twenty-four hours after viewing.

What's a +5 file? I asked.

And here's what popped up on the screen a couple of seconds later:

Come on, Jason. Figure it out.

So that was kind of snarky and personal. But not as snarky and personal as what followed.

After picking at something on my chin and thinking for a while, I realized that "+5" must refer to the recordings of the future, which were five years ahead of now. You knew that as soon as you saw it, right? I triumphantly typed:

The recordings of the future?

And here's the response I got:

Right. See? You're not such a dork after all.

chapter
27

IT WAS NOW FOUR O'CLOCK AND I HAD TO GET THE
key back to the office. I was (a) relieved that the file with
my humiliation on it would be auto-deleted by this time
tomorrow and (b) annoyed at being insulted by a help
screen that referred to itself as a T.W.E.R.P. I shut the laptop down, locked up, returned the key, and headed home.

I was halfway up my front walk when something
occurred to me. "You're not such a dork after all," the
screen had said. *After all.* Didn't that imply that I was usually considered a dork? It did. But "dork" wasn't among the
D-names my peers tended to use. "Doofus," yes. "Dweeb,"
of course. "Doorknob," sometimes. But not "dork." No,
"dork" was a word that was used to describe me by only
one person: my little sister, Alice Sloan.

So how did a help screen know that my sister had

spent almost a month calling me a dork in an ever-more-disturbing series of performances? In the past three days alone, my parents and I had been subjected to *Hickory Dickory Dork*, *Dork Whittington and His Cat*, and *The Little White Dork*. My heart was lunging around in my chest like it was looking for the emergency exit by the time I ran up the steps to my house and opened the door. I was thinking about spy cams and spy satellites and all kinds of spy other things.

I ducked into the house and shut the door behind me. I leaned on the closed door, relieved for a tiny instant before understanding that the spyware would have to be *inside the house* to have spied on the whole dork thing. There was nowhere to hide.

By the time I'd gotten up to my room, dropped my backpack, and taken off my sneakers, I had managed a few deep breaths and stopped feeling like my heart was trying to leave my body. There were no cameras in my house spying on our after-dinner "entertainment." It was just a coincidence that the Prescient help screen had used the word "dork." It had nothing to do with Alice. "Dork" was probably the word the Prescient inventor's friends had used back in the olden days when they were in school. It didn't mean anything. Or so I told myself at the time. And so I believed for as long as I could afterward.

Whatever Alice's show plans for that evening were, they were disrupted by a phone call. For me.

The phone in the kitchen rang, and Alice ran to answer it. She was the only person in the house who enjoyed talking on the phone.

"Hello, this is Alice speaking, how may I help you?" she said. "Hi, Steeeeeeve," she crooned a moment later, her voice moving up into a whole new register. Alice had a huge crush on Steve, and he was a good sport about it. He got plenty of practice. "How are you today? How do you like your new school?" Alice continued. "Jason? Jason Sloan? . . . I'm not sure he can come to the phone right now. He's in the bathroom. He might be a while. I hear grunting."

This could be a problem someday, I knew. In the unlikely event that a girl called me before I got my own phone, I was going to be sorry I hadn't nipped this behavior in the bud. But as my dad always said, with Alice you had to pick your battles. And this one wasn't worth fighting. Yet.

I wandered into the kitchen and yanked the phone out of Alice's grasp.

"Beat it," I said to her. "Sorry about that," I said into the phone.

"She's a piece of work," said Steve.

"She's a piece of something," I agreed.

"*You're* a piece of something!" Alice yelled from somewhere outside the kitchen.

"Anyway," said Steve. "I've been thinking about this whole future thing. You know? H.A.I.R. Club?"

"Uh-huh," I said.

"Well, I hate to say it, but I'm starting to think Hoppy's right. That those recordings do show the future. Do you agree with that or no?"

"Yes," I said. "I mean, I do agree." How could I not? The help screen had clinched it.

"So you know what that means," Steve said.

"Not really." I knew all too well what it meant for me and my neck and my social life and my self-respect. But I wasn't sure what it meant for Steve. Except I did, actually.

"I'm worried about my hair," he said. And I had to admire him for coming out and saying it. If someone could be unselfconsciously vain, then that's what Steve was.

He went on: "I'm sure it's a product of some kind that's making it look so . . ."

"Rubbery?" I supplied.

"Yeah. And if I know me, and I do, the product that's causing the, ah, rubbery-ness is in my locker. In the future," he added, just to be sure I was following him. And, sadly, I was.

"So?" I asked.

"I need to find out what it is. That way I can avoid it," he said.

"Can't you just not use any hair products?"

Steve barked out a laugh. "No. I need to identify this one and make sure I never use it."

"What if it's not invented yet?"

"Then I need to keep away from it when it is."

"What are you suggesting?" I asked. Because he was

definitely suggesting something. Something he needed help with. My help.

"The future recordings are only in the cafeteria, right?" he said.

"Right. As far as we know."

"So the cameras in the cafeteria must be the ones that do it."

That made so little sense that I didn't know how to begin to deny it. And Steve, being Steve, took my puzzled silence for agreement.

"So what I'm *suggesting*," he continued, "is that we exchange one of the cafeteria cameras for the one near my locker in the main hall. Then, when I open my locker in the future, I'll be able to look inside it. In the past, I mean. Or the present. Or whatever."

"But . . ." Where did I even begin? I decided to start small. Really small. "But the recordings of the future don't show that much detail. How would you be able to read the label on a bottle in your locker?"

"I've already thought about that. I must be using an economy-size drum to get my hair so . . . solid. The thing will be huge. I'll spot it. I have to."

"Okay . . . but"—I was grasping for any thin strand of sense now—"what if you only used whatever it was once, and it did something to your hair that won't wash out? Doesn't that seem more likely than you using something over and over that makes your hair look like a rubber wig?"

I thought I was presenting a logical argument, but

Steve and logic had clearly parted ways well before he got on the phone that evening.

"One dose of something could never permanently alter my hair" was his response. "My hair has too much natural resistance."

I was gathering my big argument against the whole idea that a camera could record the future when he pulled out the following: "You're my friend, right?"

That kind of question never leads anywhere good, does it? On TV, it always ends in jail time after some kind of amateur crime caper gone wrong. But then I thought about future me, who didn't seem to be friends with Steve at all anymore.

"Yes, I am," I said firmly. "Which is why—"

"So do this for me. Sunday afternoon. I'll get the key again, we'll go in, we'll switch the cameras. We can switch them back later—after we look at the recording."

I didn't like that nonspecific "later." I didn't like switching cameras while also trespassing. I didn't like any of it. But I did like Steve. I was his friend, I wanted to remain his friend, and he needed me.

"Okay," I said. "Can we bring Vincent, too?"

"Sure," said Glamorous Steve, like he was the one doing *me* a favor.

Chapter
28

WHAT HAPPENED ON SUNDAY AFTERNOON GOT STEVE, Vincent, and me into the *Flounder Bay Times*, but not for any of the reasons that might occur to you. And it could have been worse. So, so much worse.

We made it inside the school building with no trouble. No one saw us. No one was around. Who in their right mind would be hanging around the empty school on a Sunday afternoon?

And if you're expecting some wacky comedic description of the three of us and the tall stepladder that the janitors used to replace light bulbs, you're going to be disappointed. No one carrying the ladder turned abruptly and knocked anyone over, then turned to see what happened and knocked someone else over. Although Steve did manage to bash my knee with the thing and also ram Vincent in the tailbone.

None of us was in a great mood by the time we got the ladder into position under the security camera in the back left corner of the cafeteria. We chose that one because it was out of the way and less likely to be missed if we dropped it or broke it and couldn't put it back.

Vincent and I were making Steve do the hard work for obvious reasons. This was his mission—we were just muscle. And very little of that. He had to climb almost to the top of the ladder to reach the camera. Vincent and I stood by underneath to steady the ladder and be fallen on if Steve lost his balance.

"It's totally wired in here," Steve complained when he'd had a moment up there to assess the situation.

"Duh," said Vincent. His tailbone was still pretty sore. "What did you think?"

"I was thinking it would be wireless," said Steve. "What is this, the Middle Ages?"

"Don't get yourself electrocuted up there," I said insincerely. My knee was still pretty sore. "Maybe we should forget it."

"No, it's okay," Steve said after pulling tentatively on some wires. "It's just plugged in in a couple places—it's not like defusing a bomb or anything."

"That's a relief," said Vincent.

"I've got it," said Steve. "I'm handing it down to you now."

"We can see that."

The camera was remarkably light and compact. There

were two wires dangling from it, but the plugs were different enough that I didn't think we'd have a problem attaching it to the mount in the main hall.

Steve came down off the ladder and folded it up.

"Now to make the big switcheroo," he said happily. "You know what I'm thinking?" he added, catching Vincent in the elbow with the ladder.

"That I'm going to grab that ladder and bonk you over the head with it?" said Vincent.

"Nope. I'm thinking that if we were watching a recording of the future right now, we'd be seeing my hair going back to normal before our very eyes. Because right now we're taking steps to make that happen."

"I don't think that's the way it works," I said.

"The future works in mysterious ways," said Steve.

In the main hall, Steve parked the ladder under the camera nearest to his locker. He climbed up and then turned.

"Hand me the camera," he said.

I did.

"I can't unplug the other one with this one in my hand," Steve said.

Vincent and I looked at each other through the ladder's rungs and rolled our eyes.

"Hand it back to me," I said.

He did.

"Now unplug the other one and hand it to Vincent."

"Okay, okay, I've got it figured out now," said Steve.

He handed the hall camera down to Vincent and took the cafeteria camera from me.

"Wait," he said. "How do I know this is the right one?"

And so it went for several more lines of dialogue that I will spare you.

Vincent and I slumped against a wall in the main hall, heads resting against the concrete, legs outstretched, while Steve returned the ladder to the janitors' domain in the basement.

"You don't think there's any way this is going to work, do you?" Vincent asked me.

"Nope," I said. "There are so many things wrong with Steve's theory that I don't know where to begin."

Vincent waited for me to begin.

"First of all," I began, "it doesn't make sense that we have magic cameras in the cafeteria that record the future for an hour every day."

"Well, if they're not magic, what are they?"

"They're normal. Well, super-state-of-the-art normal. It's not the cameras that do it. Remember what Andrew said when we first started thinking the recordings showed the future?"

"Not particularly. A lot of what Andrew says goes over my head." Vincent made a whizzing noise and brushed a hand across the top of his hair to demonstrate.

"He said that the idea of digital files traveling through time was theoretically interesting."

"So?"

"So the cameras are just cameras. And the files of the future are files that were recorded in the future."

"That *will be* recorded in the future, you mean."

"Right. Except in the original future, they didn't have cameras as good as these." I was swimming way out of my depth here, and we both knew it.

"Original future?" Vincent repeated.

"You know . . . the future where we didn't have the Prescient stuff and didn't see our future selves."

Vincent was doing the whizzing-over-his-head thing again, only more urgently.

"Argh!" I dragged my hands down my face. "Why is this so hard to figure out?"

"We're in seventh grade," Vincent said. "We're not supposed to be able to figure everything out."

"You're right. We don't even take physics until high school. Anyway," I went on, "my theory is that someone in the original future figured out how to send those files back in time. Someone who took physics, obviously."

"Cool," said Vincent.

"Cool," I agreed.

"But why?" said Vincent a moment later. "Why, if you invented this technology that let you send recordings back in time, would you pick a lunch period at Flounder Bay Upper School and send them to the H.A.I.R. Club that you yourself set up?"

"I can't think of any reason to do that," I admitted.

chapter

29

IT WAS WHEN STEVE RETURNED FROM THE BASEMENT
that things got interesting.

"Look who I woke up down there," he said.

"Penelope!" said Vincent.

Sure enough, there was a skunk trotting behind Steve.

"She's not trapped?" I asked.

"Guess not," said Steve. "She has eluded her would-be captors."

Penelope was now butting my elbow with her head like a cat that wants to be fed or let out or some other cat-related desire. I petted her a bit and she got on my lap and settled down.

"She really likes you," Steve observed.

"We should put her in one of the traps," I said. "So Ranger Rick can pick her up."

"We could put her in one of the traps and bring her over now," said Vincent. "That way she won't have to spend the night in a trap."

"She'd be okay overnight," I said. "She'd have snacks in there."

Vincent was shaking his head. "It's a short walk, and what else do we have going on?"

We had nothing else going on.

The problem was that we couldn't find any of the traps they'd set out.

"Maybe the janitors moved them around," said Steve when we'd looked in the spots he and Vincent remembered (or thought they remembered) putting traps in.

"Or maybe you don't know where you put them," I said.

"We can carry her," said Vincent.

And by "we" he meant me, her good friend Jason.

So we let ourselves out the gym door and started off for the nature museum, me cradling the skunk like a baby in my arms.

It was fine until we got to the main road, where the sun was bright and there were cars whizzing by. Not a skunk-friendly environment. Penelope got nervous and started clawing at the front of my shirt. Cars slowed down as the people in them gawked at the kid carrying a skunk.

Then Penelope got so nervous she clawed her way up onto my shoulder, and that's when a car pulled over and a guy yelled out the window, "Do you need help?"

Another car pulled over and a lady got out. The first guy yelled over at her, "That kid's being attacked by a skunk!"

"She's not atta—" I managed, but they weren't about to consult with me in this emergency.

"It's probably rabid," said the woman. "It wouldn't be out in daylight if it were healthy." She had pulled out her phone.

So had the guy. "I'm calling Animal Control," he said. "Hang in there, kid. Don't make any sudden moves."

"I'm okay," I said. "She's a tame—"

But it was no use. The guy was making the call, the woman was either taking pictures or video, and a third car had pulled over.

"You other kids need to back away," said the original guy to Vincent and Steve. "We don't want it attacking you too."

And you know what? Steve and Vincent, who knew perfectly well that Penelope was not rabid and not attacking me, did as they were told.

And then the Animal Control van swerved into place behind the three spectator cars. The doors opened and two people in khaki got out. They went over to talk to the guy and the woman, eyeing me the whole time without getting any closer.

"We surrender!" Vincent yelled from his backed-away position. He had his hands up.

The Animal Control officers ignored him.

There was another woman here now, with a fancy camera, taking pictures from what she must have thought was a safe distance.

None of this, by the way, was making Penelope any less nervous. She was standing on my shoulder with her claws digging into me, and although it didn't qualify as an attack, it wasn't comfortable. I decided that the best thing to do was keep walking. We weren't that far from the museum.

"Stop!" called one of the Animal Control officers as soon as I'd taken a couple of steps.

"Don't move, kid," called the other one. "Stay calm and we'll get it sedated, okay? Hang in there; you're doing great."

People say this kind of stuff to women giving birth in their cars by the side of the road all the time, but it wasn't helpful here. And in fact, it probably isn't that helpful to the women giving birth either.

"It's okay," I said. "She's tame. She's a tame skunk. We're taking her to the natural history museum. They've been looking for her."

For a moment I was stunned that I'd been able to get this out without some adult interruption.

"You mean Penelope?" asked the Animal Control woman.

"Yes!" I said. "Penelope, from the natural history museum."

The two officers exchanged glances.

And now that we had *that* straightened out, I prepared to be on my way.

Until: "Kid," said the woman, "I hate to be the one to tell you this, but Penelope came back to the museum on her own. I don't know who that skunk is, but it's not Penelope."

chapter
30

AND THAT'S HOW I CAME TO BE CALLED SKUNK BOY for several days in school and for weeks in my own home.

Alice's Dork series was replaced by a long-running and very popular show called *The Adventures of Skunk Boy*, featuring me and a skunk puppet that she happened to have handy. Even Dad thought it was hilarious.

My picture appeared in the town paper the following week, below the headline "Local Boy in Skunk Attack." And I have to admit that I looked like a total dork in the photo, standing there cluelessly beneath this obviously freaked-out skunk. Alice pinned it up on her bulletin board.

The skunk wasn't rabid—just disoriented from being woken up during the day. The Animal Control people sneaked up behind it and tranquilized it right there on my shoulder. No one asked where we'd found it—I think they assumed it had launched itself at me there on the street. Anyway, it went to live at the natural history museum until they were sure it was healthy. They named it Jason, to my sister's delight.

So yes, the skunk got to be called Jason and I got to be called Skunk Boy. Funny how that worked.

In case you're curious about whether Steve's experiment with the cameras succeeded, the answer is no, it did not. When the camera from the cafeteria was moved to the main hall, it recorded the main hall in the present, not the future. This was a blow for Steve.

"What am I going to do now?" he said when we'd watched the midnight recordings from the main hall and the cafeteria (present in main hall, future in cafeteria, as usual). He ran a hand through his doomed hair.

"Give up?" Hoppy said unsympathetically. "Let's face it. Assuming these images are our future—and we all do, right?" Everyone nodded. "The future doesn't look that good for most of us." Hoppy was at the controls, and she started moving around the cafeteria, darting toward each of us in turn as she narrated our fates. "I look exactly like my mother. And I'm acting like her too. Do you see what I'm doing here? I'm telling the servers in the cafeteria how to set up the food trays more efficiently."

"You are," said Andrew. "And they're doing it."

"Of course they are," said Hoppy. "And look at Sonia!

She's obviously dealing with some personal stuff by constantly changing fashions and boys."

"Hey!" said Sonia. But she shook her head as we watched her future self sitting on the lap of a kid whose facial hair made future Nikhil's look dignified. Both of them were wearing mismatched plaid clothing with all kinds of chains attached at various points. They looked like they might be chained together, or at least hard to pull apart in a hurry.

"Wow," Sonia said. "I'm dressed like a set of bagpipes. My parents might be strict and all, but seriously—this is how I act out? Moving from one weird style to another and accessorizing with a different matching boy? And what am I doing with the old, out-of-style boys? Stashing their bodies in the cafeteria freezer?"

"Don't worry about that," Hoppy said bitterly. "I've probably got the freezer so well organized you'd never be able to hide anything in there."

Hoppy resumed her pitiless tour of our futures. "Poor Vincent. Whatever candle he's burning at both ends is about to burn out. And there's Jason. Talking with his mouth full and staring into space."

It wasn't space I was staring at, but I wasn't going to point that out.

"Nikhil trying to look like a man with that moth-eaten mustache," Hoppy continued. "Andrew undermining his own college choice. Steve's hair gel from hell. Face it," she wound up. "The only winner here seems to be Lara."

And she zoomed in on the tall blonde standing inside the doorway.

No one said anything for a moment. I'm fairly certain that only Hoppy, Lara, and I knew this incredibly cool vision was Lara. And it's a good thing I did know, because if I hadn't, there's a strong chance I would have gasped and then blurted out something like "There's no way that fabulous person could be Lara!" No one, including me, did that out loud, fortunately. But some of them were definitely thinking it.

It wasn't that future Lara was gorgeous in any kind of artificial way. But she somehow gave the impression that there was a special spotlight on her, the kind of spotlight that seems to follow celebrities around even when they're hurrying through airports or trying to avoid photographers in dingy alleys. She seemed to be in charge of herself in a way that hardly any teenager has a right to be.

"So what do we do?" asked Sonia. "Is this it? Are we stuck with this future?"

"No," said Steve. "We can't be. This is *a* future, not *the* future. I mean, Nikhil has already ditched the whole mustache idea, right?"

"So why do I still have one here?" Nikhil asked gloomily. "Why hasn't the future changed now that I've changed my mind?"

chapter
31

"THERE MUST BE A WAY TO FIGURE OUT HOW THIS works," said Hoppy.

"We could try the help screen," I said, not volunteering that I had already tried it and been insulted by it.

"Help screens are no help," said Nikhil.

We all knew this, but we also knew that there were no other options.

"Here it is," said Hoppy. "It's called a T.W.E.R.P. screen. Which is on-brand. What do you want to know?"

"You know what we want to know," said Steve.

"That's what the help screen is asking," said Hoppy. "It doesn't list topics or anything. It just says 'What do you want to know?'"

What *did* we want to know, exactly?

Different things, it turned out.

"What's wrong with my hair?" Steve.

"Why do I look like a zombie?" Vincent.

"What happened to my good taste?" Sonia.

"Why do I still have that mustache?" Nikhil.

"Yo!" shouted Hoppy above the anguished cries for answers. "How about 'Can we change the future?'"

"That seems like a general philosophical question, not a help-screen-type question," said Andrew.

"Well, this is a smart program," said Hoppy, typing in what she'd said. She then shifted what was on the laptop to the big screen so we could all see.

Sorry! popped up in the answer window. **That question is outside the parameters of this system. Please try something else.**

"Told you," said Andrew. "It can't answer G.P.Q.s."

"Huh?" said Vincent.

"General philosophical questions," said Andrew.

"Oh, right," said Vincent. "G.P.Q.s. Of course."

"Be more specific," said Steve to Hoppy.

Hoppy sighed forcefully. "All right," she said. "Here goes."

Why does Steve's hair look like a plastic dog turd in the future? she typed.

"Specific enough for you?" she asked Steve.

"There's no need to be cruel," said Steve. But he was staring intently at the screen.

Which came back with the same canned response about parameters.

"I guess it's not that smart after all," said Vincent.

"What I don't understand," said Hoppy, "is how it knows my name but it can't at least try to answer a question like this."

"What do you mean it knows your name?" Nikhil asked.

"When I first clicked on the help screen, it used my name," said Hoppy.

"That's because we all registered with our names the first day," said Andrew. "And you logged on as yourself, right?"

"Right," said Hoppy. "But I registered as Harriet. And when I opened the help screen, it said, 'Hello, Hoppy.'"

"Weird," Steve said.

"But not that weird," said Andrew. "It also threatened to release those butt-ugly photos of us on the Internet, right? So it must have access to your social media stuff, Hoppy. Maybe that's where it got your nickname."

"But that's what I mean," said Hoppy. "Why would it bother to search around and find my nickname when it could call me Harriet? Or not call me anything."

"You're thinking that it's smarter than it needs to be," said Andrew.

"Exactly," said Hoppy. "So why can't it answer a G.P.Q. about the future? Or a specific one about Steve's hair?"

"You would think," said Steve when we'd stewed for a while, "that if it has access to our social media, it would at least come back with something like 'That does not compute'"—and yes, he did say this in a fake robot voice, exactly like you're picturing—"when Hoppy typed 'Steve's hair' and 'dog turd' in the same sentence. Am I right?"

He was right. More right than he knew. This was a program that had chatted with me like an old friend, or at least like my sister, when I'd asked it questions. Why was it acting like a machine now?

Maybe I had managed to goad the T.W.E.R.P. screen into insulting me by badgering it with questions. I tried to remember exactly what I had asked, thinking Hoppy could get it to insult her too. Or at least admit that it knew something about the future.

I racked my brain and finally said, "Ask it what a plus-five file is." I did remember that much from last week.

"Why?" more than one person asked.

"Because that's what it calls the future files. Plus sign and the numeral five."

"How do you know that?" Nikhil asked. Kind of pointedly.

"I, ah, I asked it some questions last week. When you guys were skunk trapping."

Lara was looking at me like I was Steve's future hair. Only not plastic. I avoided her gaze the way she used to avoid mine.

"What the heck," said Hoppy, typing away.

What is a +5 file?

The answer came back quickly, and let's just say parameters were mentioned again.

"I guess it likes you better than me," said Hoppy.

"Maybe *Jason* should type it," Lara said. And it was probably my imagination, but it seemed to me that she said it in the way a pirate would say "Maybe *Jason* should walk the plank."

So I sat down at the other laptop, logged in, and clicked on the red question mark.

Hello, Jason. What do you want to know?

"No surprise there," said Vincent. "Jason doesn't have a nickname."

At least it hadn't called me a dork. Yet.

What is a +5 file? I typed.

Sorry! That question is outside the parameters of this system. Please try something else.

chapter

32

THE ENTIRE H.A.I.R. CLUB WAS LOOKING AT ME LIKE
I was a few fins short of a flounder. And maybe I was.
Maybe I had hallucinated the whole help-screen exchange
before.

I shrugged and said, "Maybe I hallucinated the whole
thing. Sorry."

Which deflated any accusations they had been getting
ready to throw at me.

Except: "Seems like a weirdly detailed hallucination,"
said Nikhil.

No one else said anything. I was pretty sure Lara's eyes
were calling me a lying piece of dog toupee, but I wasn't
going to test that theory.

"We're out of time," Steve said eventually.

He didn't mean that our disappointing futures were

set in stone and there was nothing we could do about it, but can we be blamed for taking it that way and slouching dejectedly out of the room?

Probably we can, actually. I mean, our fates didn't look *that* depressing. We were overprivileged American kids whose tiny problems were laughable to the vast majority of Earth's population, now and five years in the future. I get that. But we were still left with a question that anyone can sympathize with. If we didn't like the way our futures were shaping up—and almost none of us did—could we change them, or were we stuck with what we were seeing?

Nikhil, to take a simple example, had decided not to grow a mustache. But was he somehow destined to grow one in spite of that? Maybe he was going to develop a skin condition on his upper lip that could only be cured by not shaving. Or maybe his dad would act all hurt that Nikhil didn't want to follow in his facial-hair footsteps and guilt Nikhil into growing it.

Or, to take a more complex example, maybe I was destined to have a crush on Lara even though, at the moment, I was plain terrified of her. It was already clear that she was destined to dislike me strongly for all time.

These questions bothered me for the first part of my walk home, but my brain felt like it was overheating and maybe starting to bubble, so I switched to a topic that was easier to think about, even if I still had no answers. Which was why the help screen had treated me like a stranger today. I was almost sure I had asked it the same question as before, but this time I'd gotten the cold shoulder instead of a warm personal insult. Something must have been different.

The only difference I could think of was that the other time I'd been alone. Maybe the help screen was a bully, picking on people when there was no one there to defend them. Not that anyone in that room would have defended me—they would have piled on and enjoyed themselves while they were at it. And that didn't explain why it had been at all helpful the first time. Bullies aren't ever helpful as a rule. Being the opposite of helpful is more their thing.

By the time I got home, I had faced the fact that these questions were way out of my league technologically. Up in my room, I sat down at my laptop and thought about googling the problem, but I couldn't figure out how to word it.

There was only one thing left to try: the Family Help Desk, as we called her. I e-mailed Aunt Shannon.

There's something weird going on with the H.A.I.R. Club help screen, I wrote. **I asked it a question the other day and got a detailed answer. I asked it the same question today and it said, basically, "That does not compute." The only difference was that I was alone the first day and I was with the whole club today. The program knows who's there. What do you think happened?**

I didn't know what Aunt Shannon did all day at work, but she almost always answered her e-mails immediately. Sometimes before there'd been enough time to type. At least the way I type. So I didn't have to wait long for a reply.

Wow. Your Prescient Technologies mystery gets even more mysterious! I'm going to have to mull this over. In the meantime, has anyone else had the same experience?

I replied: No, just me. No one else has been alone with it as far as I know. And when Hoppy asked the same question with everyone there, she got the non-response too.

She replied: Scientifically speaking, you should try the same question again when you're alone, and Hoppy (or someone else) should do the same. Then you'll have some real data.

I don't suppose you'd care to share with me what the question was?

I sat back in my chair. I should have known she'd be curious. I should have thought about how much I wanted to tell her before I e-mailed her. And about how much the other club members would want me to tell her. I couldn't remember if the mile-long user agreement allowed us to talk to others about what we saw on those screens, even just the help one. I certainly had no desire to reread it to find out.

I borrowed a phrase from Shannon and wrote back:

I'm going to have to mull that over.

chapter
33

BUT THAT MULLING HAD TO WAIT, BECAUSE I GOT some unasked-for help from an unexpected source.

First, some background on my uncle Luke. As I've mentioned, he is my mother's baby brother. He is also kind of a baby, period, especially when it comes to his health.

Uncle Luke, who worked at home by himself, tended to fixate on any bodily sensation or weirdness that caught his attention. My mom claimed he once called her at 3:00 a.m. because a hangnail was "pulsating." She told him where to put his pulsating hangnail.

So he'd always been bad, but it got way worse after Woozle came along. Now that he had Woozle, he could look up any tiny thing that occurred to him and then click on Images, and then freak out and call my mother. Keep in mind that my mother was a bookseller with no medical training—but she was his big sister and she tended to be able to talk him down.

The next day when I got home from school, my mother and Alice were in the driveway. My mother had her "medical kit," which was a ziplock containing a handful of Band-Aids, a tube of antiseptic, and a paper bag for Luke to breathe in when he was panicked and started panting.

"Get in the car," she said as I walked into earshot.

"Seriously?"

"He got his ear pierced and thinks he's got an infection that's going to his brain."

"*Something* has gone to his brain," I muttered.

"*You've* gone to his brain," said Alice.

"What does that mean?"

"Nothing to *you*."

When we arrived at Luke and Shannon's house, we found Luke lying on the sofa.

"You're fine," said my mom, barely glancing at him.

"My ear's hot, and I think there are red streaks going down the side of my neck, and I'm dizzy and disoriented," Luke whined.

"Here's your bag," said Mom.

Luke sat up, took the paper bag, and started breathing into it.

"Why did you get your ear pierced anyway?" Mom asked.

"Just felt like it," Luke mumbled into his bag.

"It's because you turned thirty, isn't it? Feeling a little less hip than you'd like?"

Luke put the bag aside. "I think I'm okay," he said, pushing himself to a stand. "Look at my ear, though. It feels like it's on fire."

"It's a little red," my mom said after no more than two seconds of inspection. "But that's normal right after you get it pierced. You can't drive a metal spike through a piece of flesh and not expect a little irritation."

Luke's face turned ghastly white. "Oh my god," he moaned. And down he went.

"At least he landed on the sofa," I pointed out.

"Put his feet up on a pillow," said Mom. "I'm going to call Shannon. Where's my phone?"

"At home on the counter," said Alice helpfully.

"Where's Luke's phone?"

We looked around and didn't see it.

My mother sighed. "Would it kill them to have a land-line? Check his office, Jason. Alice, that's way too many pillows."

Luke's "office" was a portion of the basement that he had walled off, mainly with junk. He did something with computers, but that was all I knew. I walked through the kitchen and downstairs into the basement. I looked around his messy desk for his phone and didn't see it. Then I checked the other likely surfaces. I was about to give up and go back upstairs when I saw several flat cardboard boxes tucked in vertically beside his desk.

Something about them caught my eye.

And that something was two words, printed on the first one:

PRESCIENT TECHNOLOGIES

chapter

34

"NEVER MIND ABOUT THE PHONE, JASON," CAME MOM'S voice from upstairs. "It was in his pocket."

By that time I was pawing through those boxes like they were going to tell me something important. They didn't. They all had the Prescient name on them, but nothing helpful like an address or a website. I sat down on Luke's ratty office chair to think.

The boxes hadn't been used—no tape shreds, no labels—so Luke hadn't gotten something in the mail *from* Prescient. This was weirder. It looked like he was the mail*er*, not the mail*ee*.

I'm not proud of what I did next, but this history hasn't really been about things I'm proud of up to this point, so why should that change now?

I started shuffling through the piles of paper on his

desk, looking for anything else with Prescient on it. If he had boxes, maybe he had envelopes or stationery or a business card.

He did not.

Then I went beyond casual snooping and entered the territory of outright prying. I opened the file drawer of the desk. I thumbed through his files, which were (sort of surprisingly) in perfect alphabetical order. And there it was: a big fat file folder labeled "Prescient" in Luke's sloppy printing. I was about to move beyond outright prying and enter into some creepy CIA-ish realm of actual spying when Alice appeared in the doorway and bellowed, "We're leaving now. I have a tap lesson. What are you *doing*? *MOM!*"

I closed the desk drawer and leaped away from the desk, as if I'd look less guilty by putting some distance between me and it.

"Nothing" was my brilliant comeback.

Fortunately, Mom was in no mood to listen to Alice's latest grievance. Shannon was on her way home to deal with Luke, and Alice was late for tap. We practically burned rubber out of the driveway.

Let me state for the historical record that Alice Sloan was one mean tap dancer. In both senses of the word "mean." That she was mean in the nasty sense should surprise no one who has been reading this entire history and not skipping the Alice sections. Here are some of the things she said to her fellow students of tap, while they were dancing:

"Faster, Jessica! This isn't ballet."

"Are those arms or noodles, Ellie?"

"You're supposed to tap, not stomp, [name redacted to protect the victim's privacy]!"

The teacher intervened with that last one, but Alice waved her off. Or was she doing jazz hands? I couldn't tell.

Mom just sat there behind the non-soundproof glass in the studio, reading a book. When she finally looked up, toward the end of the class, all she did was smile at me and say, "That kid can dance, can't she?"

"Who knew there was trash-talking in tap class?" I said.

My oblivious parent chuckled and went back to her book.

Meanwhile, when I wasn't being simultaneously horrified and impressed by Alice, I was thinking hard about the whole Luke-Prescient thing. I arrived at a few conclusions. Among them:

- Luke either worked for or in fact was the mysterious "entrepreneur" behind Prescient Technologies.
- Luke probably just worked for this person. I simply could not picture my goofy uncle as some kind of tech genius.
- Luke hadn't told Shannon about this job. I concluded this because I was sure Shannon

149

would have mentioned it when I talked to
her about Prescient.

- If Luke hadn't told Shannon about it,
  it's because he'd been instructed not to.
  Luke was almost filterless, especially with
  Shannon.
- So Luke secretly worked for a company that
  (a) had access to future security recordings
  of the Flounder Bay Upper School cafeteria
  and (b) seemed to want the H.A.I.R. Club to
  see them.

The main question was still *why* it wanted us to see
them. But that was only one of the many, many questions
I now had.

My final conclusion was this:

- Luke needed to be pumped for information,
  and Shannon needed to be there when he
  was.

chapter
35

WHAT HAPPENED NEXT MIGHT SURPRISE YOU AS MUCH as it surprised me. Because things haven't tended to go right for me so far in this history. But now, two things did in a row.

First, my mom decided to swing by after Alice's class and see how Luke's brain infection was coming along.

Second, when we got there, Alice insisted that it was her "turn" to play on Luke's swivel chair, "because Jason was hogging it earlier." My mom went down with her to make sure she didn't spin so hard she puked.

So there I was, alone with Luke and Shannon. Exactly what I wanted. Now was my chance to stop dithering, to take charge and move this investigation forward. The problem was how to begin. I wasn't one to just sit down with a couple of adults and start chatting.

Shannon was perched on the very end of the sofa, which Luke was still flopped on. He had an ice pack on his earlobe and kept asking her to check if he was getting frostbite. I was in the armchair opposite, drinking a caffeinated soda my mother didn't know about and working up some liquid courage.

"So, Jason," said Shannon, when she'd assured Luke his earlobe wasn't turning white or blue or any other color that meant frostbite, "any progress on the H.A.I.R. Club mystery?"

This got the conversational ball rolling in the right direction, anyway. Now I just needed to kick it into the goal. Which I managed as awkwardly as I possibly could have. I remembered each and every word for the historical record because I kept replaying them in my head and hearing how dumb they sounded.

"No," I said, my eyes on Luke. "I can't figure out what's going on with *Prescient Technologies.*"

Yup. That was me, Jason Sloan, Expert Interrogator, raking my uncle over the coals. I looked so hard at him I was kind of squinting and waited for him to crack.

The weird thing is, he did.

He tried to meet my penetrating gaze for a second or two. But he couldn't hold it. He looked away, first at the ceiling, then at Shannon, then at the TV, which wasn't on.

I upped the intensity of my laser-like focus on him. If my eyes had been real lasers, his whole face would have needed that ice pack. And he felt it—oh yes, he felt it. He moved the ice pack over his eyes.

"Luke, what are you doing?" Shannon asked. "You're going to freeze your eyeballs."

"Can that happen?" asked Luke, yanking the ice away.

"I don't know," said Shannon.

"I'll woozle it," said Luke, grabbing for his phone.

"What? No!" said Shannon. "We were talking to Jason about his club. Don't be rude."

"So, yeah," I said, leaning back fake casually. "I feel like I need to know more about *Prescient Technologies*, but there's nothing out there. I mean, *who are they*?"

Luke went to clap the ice pack over his eyes again, but he was still holding his phone, and he accidentally clunked that onto his face instead. It was not his finest moment.

Did I mention that Shannon is smart? She is, and she knows her husband really well. "Are you okay?" she asked him when he'd put the phone down on the coffee table and the ice pack on the wrong ear. Then, without waiting for a response, she said, "Prescient Technologies."

He flinched like she'd flicked him.

"Prescient Technologies!"

He flinched again, like she'd slapped him.

"Luke," she said, "is there something you want to share with the class?"

He groaned and put a pillow over his face.

"We can still see you."

"I can't talk about it," he said through the pillow.

"It's only us, honey. Your loving wife and your adorable nephew."

"I can't" came through the pillow.

Shannon looked at me and shrugged.

The adorable nephew shrugged back.

"Why can't you?" she asked Luke gently.

He removed the pillow from his face and hugged it like a stuffed animal. "There's an extremely aggressive confidentiality agreement," he said. "And they have a picture of me. . . ."

"They have one of me, too!" I said.

"They could also come after me legally," said Luke. "In ways I don't like to think about."

"So you both signed a confidentiality agreement with Prescient?" said Shannon.

We nodded.

"Doesn't that mean you can talk to each other?"

I told you she was smart.

chapter
36

SHANNON LEFT THE ROOM SO LUKE AND I COULD discuss Prescient freely.

Which got awkward right away.

"So, ah, you know about Prescient Technologies?" I began. Jason Sloan, Expert Interrogator, had left the building. Caffeine will only get you so far.

"Uh, yeah. I've done some work for them. And you know about them too?"

"Yeah. That's what we do in H.A.I.R. Club. Monitor the security stuff they gave the school."

We both looked longingly at the TV, which still wasn't on.

"So who are they?" I asked him.

Luke shrugged while holding the pillow to his chest and the ice pack to the wrong ear. "I don't know. They approached me in a very roundabout way with this weird proposition. It's not like they're evil or anything. Just secretive. Not, like, spy secretive. Just . . . I don't know."

"So what did you do for them?" I asked.

"I put together some equipment, based on their specs, and shipped it to the school."

"You built that stuff? The laptops and screens and stuff?"

He shrugged again. "That's what I do. Their designs, though. Which were like nothing I've ever seen before."

"Wow." I should say here that I had never been the least bit curious about what Luke did for work. It had certainly never occurred to me that it was something interesting.

"Yeah," he said. "It's amazing. Almost futuristic."

I had just sipped from my soda and came close to spraying it out my nose.

Luke raised one eyebrow but didn't comment.

"So did you, like, program the laptops too?" I asked.

"I downloaded the software and files they provided."

I knew we were running out of time. Alice was going to get dizzy soon, and even if she didn't, my mother's patience wasn't endless.

"So you must have a way to get in touch with them," I said. "Right? The help screen is doing some strange stuff, and we have questions about some of the, um, files, and it would be good if we could ask them."

Luke was already shaking his head. "Sorry. The

communication has been almost entirely one way."

"But how is that possible?"

"It's complicated. They contacted me through Warren."

"I don't know who that is."

"It's not a person. It's an online game. It has to do with rabbits. I know it sounds silly, but it's really gripping when you get into it."

"What do you do?"

"Each player is a rabbit, and there are different levels of warrens. And you want to move up to the next level, but to do that you need carrots—those are the currency of Warren. So to earn carrots you have to pass these intelligence tests, and also perform various skills, and also help out other rabbits."

"Community service?"

"I guess. The more you do, the more carrots you earn, and the easier it is to get into an elite-level warren."

It sounded utterly stupid and pointless, but I nodded.

"Anyway, the Prescient people contacted me through Warren and asked me to build the one set of equipment for the school. They gave me the specs and sent the files to me through Warren. I never got any contact information, and as soon as the job was done, they disappeared."

"But they must have paid you. Didn't that have a name with it?"

Luke went really red and briefly moved his ice pack back to his eyes. Then he yanked it away and tossed it on the floor. He mumbled, "They paid me in carrots."

"Carrots?" I repeated.

"Carrots?" came a shriek from the kitchen area.

But that's when Alice puked, so I did not get to see what happened as Luke tried to explain to Shannon that he'd built all that futuristic equipment in return for a bushel of virtual vegetables.

chapter 37

I BELIEVE I MENTIONED AT THE BEGINNING OF THIS historical account that I don't rush into things. So I didn't go right to my fellow club members with this information from Luke. Instead, I opted to think it through on my own for a while. Was this this a smart decision? I'll leave that for you to decide.

What I came up with on my own was this: Whoever was behind Prescient, they were smart enough to send files from the future back in time through an online game. They knew Luke well enough to know that he played the game and that he could build the equipment. They knew me well enough to know that I would join H.A.I.R. Club at school and be called a dork at home. And finally, they seemed to want to torment me, and possibly the other club members, with disturbing glimpses of our senior year.

So they were smart, they knew my family, and they were mean.

Who did that leave, really?

Alice Sloan. That's who it left.

Laugh if you want, but for me, all indicators now pointed to my sister as the future evil genius who created Prescient Technologies.

I'm not quite as much of a fool as you are thinking I am. I knew I needed to test my theory. And the only way I could think of to do that was to go back to the T.W.E.R.P. screen and see if I could get it to admit that it was Alice.

Of all the issues I was facing, this one seemed pretty easy. If I knew anything at all, it was how to get a rise out of Alice. I'd been training for that for years. I was sure that if I could get some time alone with the help screen, I could bother it until it ran screaming for Mom. And then I would have proof. And afterward? I'd think about that when the time came.

So there I was, after school on Friday, in the office, pretending to need a bus pass. When the secretary went into the back to get the unnecessary pass from the printer, I casually took a key to the H.A.I.R. Club janitors' closet and slipped it into my pocket. Simple as that.

I didn't see anyone in the basement, and I was feeling proud as I let myself into club headquarters and carefully shut the door behind me. I put down my stuff and sat at one of the desks. I opened the laptop and prepared to get right to business. Which is when I noticed that the help screen was already up and ready to go.

"Huh," I said (out loud, to myself).

Had we left the program running since our meeting? It seemed unlikely. And wouldn't it have timed out? It had an irritating habit of doing that. All this wondering took only seconds in real time. At which point I noticed that the words on the screen weren't:

Hello, Jason. What do you want to know?

They were instead:

Hello, Lara. What do you want to know?

Lara hadn't even logged on yesterday. So why did the help screen think it was talking to her now?

"Huh," I said again (again out loud).

The important thing to remember here is that I was the club historian, not the club detective. Which is why I didn't immediately put together the fact of Lara's name on the help screen and the additional fact that I hadn't needed to unlock the door to let myself into the closet. I'm sure I would have figured out what was going on eventually. But I didn't have to.

An aggravated sigh came from under the desk I was sitting at. And then a voice asked, "Can you move back so I can get out?"

If she hadn't sighed first and at least given me that small amount of warning, I'm pretty sure I would have shrieked when she spoke. Instead I moved my chair backward so fast I skidded into the wall and knocked over a push broom left over from the closet's heyday.

I was still sitting in the chair next to the fallen broom when Lara crawled out from under the desk, looking maybe one-tenth embarrassed and all the other tenths annoyed.

"What are you doing here?" I managed as I righted the broom.

She stood up and dusted off her pants. "What does it look like?" she asked, gesturing at the help screen with her name and the blinking cursor.

"You wanted to see what happened if you asked it questions when you were alone," I said. I may be a historian and not a detective, but I'm also (possibly contrary to your opinion of me) not a complete doofus.

"*Bing*-o," said Lara in the tone of someone who disagrees strongly with the above non-doofus assessment.

Was it just me or was her whole shyness thing turning into something much snarkier?

chapter

38

"WHY WERE YOU HIDING UNDER THE DESK?" I ASKED Lara, trying to put her on the defensive.

"Because I'm not supposed to be in here," she said. "And neither are you."

So now *I* was on the defensive. That was quick. "You were hiding from *me*?"

"I thought you were Ms. Grossman."

Of course she wasn't hiding from me. What was the club historian going to do to her? Write her up in his history? Which, yes, I just did. See the effect it had? No? Exactly.

"We can't both be alone with the help screen at the same time," I observed.

Her silence was way louder than her spoken "Duh" would have been.

"And since you were here first," I babbled into the "Duh"-laden silence, "I guess I should step outside until you're done." I stood up.

"Thanks," she said, immediately taking the seat in front of the laptop.

I was turning to grab my stuff and leave when there was a rattling, trundling, janitorial noise in the corridor. We each dove under a different desk.

The noise halted outside the door. I'm pretty sure it was one of those big carts the janitors used to move cartons of toilet paper and stuff around the school. The ones that looked like they would be fun to ride on. Then there was a series of clanking noises signifying something heavy being moved. Then the cart rolled away.

Lara and I waited a few minutes under the desks until we were sure the cart and the janitor driving it were gone. Then we crawled out.

"That was close," I said, without really meaning it. A janitor had about as much power to get us in trouble in this situation as a club historian did.

"We should go," said Lara.

I nodded, but I was really thinking that *she* should go so I could move ahead with my plan.

She shut down the laptop and picked up her backpack. Then she stood next to the door, waiting for me.

I thought about saying something like "Catch you later," but I realized I couldn't do it. Lara Andersen was expecting me to leave with her, and I wasn't going to refuse. Why? Because I had a crush on her? Not at all. Because I was afraid of her.

I grabbed my backpack and then grabbed the doorknob and pulled. Nothing happened. Realizing my error, I turned the knob again and pushed. The door opened about one inch before slamming into something heavy that was right outside it. I pushed again, harder, and the heavy thing—which turned out to be the very stepladder that Steve and Vincent and I had used during the Skunk Boy episode—toppled and slammed into the wall opposite. And wedged there.

"What did you *do*?" Lara asked in that way a parent does when surveying a scene of total destruction.

I looked through the skinny glass panel in the door and saw the ladder and its position spanning the hallway from door to wall.

"Nothing! The janitor left a ladder leaning against the door, and when I opened the door, it fell against the wall. I need to push it out of the way."

I pulled the door closed and opened it again forcefully, expecting the ladder to give way. It did not. Instead, it seemed to wedge itself more firmly between the door and the wall.

"Uh-oh," I said.

"Let me try," said Lara.

She got the door open maybe two inches, then gave it a vicious kick, which did nothing to the door, though it did heighten my fear of her.

"Help me," she said.

So we both kicked the door. Over and over. Even if it didn't budge the ladder, at least the noise would attract someone. That's what I was hoping, anyway.

Then we gave up on kicking, and I started yelling through the crack in the door, "Help! Somebody help! We're trapped in the janitors' closet! Anyone?"

Lara stared at me wide-eyed as I yelled. Like she couldn't imagine ever yelling like that for any reason, but also like she was glad I was willing to do it.

After a while it seemed clear that the janitor who had left the ladder outside the door was now on his way home to his family and was not going to hear us and come to our rescue. Nor was anyone else.

"You don't happen to have a phone," I said to Lara.

She shook her head. "You?"

"Nope. Not until ninth grade."

"How did the only two kids in the whole school whose parents actually obey that stupid rule end up trapped in a janitors' closet?" said Lara.

"Vincent doesn't have one either," I said.

She just glared at me.

"I guess we could e-mail someone," I said. We had the laptops, after all.

We thought about the people we knew who might read their e-mail before one of us had to go to the bathroom. (And yes, I was very sorry that idea had entered my head.)

"I could try my aunt," I said.

"I could try my dad."

We both sat there picturing our respective adults coming to rescue us from a ladder.

"I have another idea," I said.

"Okay," said Lara immediately.

"What if we take that broom and poke it out the door and try to push the ladder sideways?"

This was a terrible idea, and we both liked it way more than e-mailing an adult and then explaining ourselves to that adult.

Since it was my idea, it seemed fair that I be the one to try to move the ladder aside with the broom.

So beneath Lara's critical gaze, I grabbed the broom as manfully as I could and poked its handle out the narrow opening of the door.

First I tried to push the legs of the ladder, which were wedged against the door. There was some undignified grunting during this attempt. But I couldn't move the broom handle around the door enough to budge anything.

Then I decided that I would reach across the hall with the broom handle and try to knock the top of the ladder aside. To do this I had to hold the very end of the broom— the actual broom part of it. Which made the whole thing very hard to control. Which is my excuse for what happened next.

Chapter
39

I TOOK ALL THE BLAME. WITH THE FIREFIGHTERS, with Ms. Grossman, with Ms. Wu, with our parents. I took all the blame because what happened was completely my fault. Except the ladder. That was *not* my fault. Who leaves a ladder in front of a door? I'm hoping now, as I write this history in the calm after the storm, that Lara maybe respected me a tiny bit because of my blame-taking.

But she wasn't respecting me as I flailed away at a wedged ladder with an out-of-control broom handle. And even that very low level of respect must have nose-dived when, instead of pushing the ladder out of the way, I somehow managed with my flailing to poke and break and also set off the fire alarm on the wall opposite, which activated the basement's sprinkler system.

The noise of the alarm was loud and scary. The water

from the sprinklers was cold and everywhere. By the time it occurred to either of us that the Prescient equipment was getting wet, it was way too late to stop screaming and cover it with any of the other dripping-wet things in the room. We grabbed the laptops and dove under the desks, but that was mostly to get ourselves out from under the sprinklers.

Soon we could hear sirens as fire trucks sped toward the school. It was sort of nice to know that in case of an actual fire, we were safe, what with the aggressive sprinklers and the immediate response from the fire department. We were grateful when the alarms were silenced and the sprinklers turned off. And we were super embarrassed when a single firefighter easily lifted the ladder out of the way with one hand and opened the door to the closet.

We crawled out from under the desks, clutching the soaked laptops, Lara close to tears and me saying "I'm so sorry, I'm so sorry" over and over again.

I'm thinking that the conversations and investigations and detentions and community service and other "repercussions" (Ms. Grossman word) that followed don't really belong in a history of H.A.I.R. Club, so I'm going to leave those to your imagination. The whole process was unpleasant and humiliating, not to mention long and tedious. I sincerely hope never to spend a weekend heaving waterlogged cases of toilet paper into a dumpster ever again.

None of that was as bad as having to explain to the other club members that because I'd sneaked into head-quarters and then panicked and then flailed, our state-of-the-art security equipment was possibly ruined. Every particle of my hard-earned skunk-petting cred went right down the tubes that afternoon, never to return.

No one seemed to blame Lara for any of this, though she had done her share of the sneaking, at least. In fact, everyone seemed to be feeling sorry for her because of her association with me, the Flounder Bay Flailer.

If you're interested in reading the minutes of that par-ticular Tuesday's club meeting, I'm sure Sonia took down every word in permanent purple ink. Every angry, insult-ing word.

So now I'd managed to alienate almost all my friends in this timeline too. Apparently I was destined to end up alone at a lunch table with Rip van Vincent no matter what I did. Toward the end of the most unpleasant meet-ing in H.A.I.R. Club history, Ms. Grossman knocked on the door and then came in without waiting for a response.

"Well," she said when she had our attention, "I've got some good news and some bad news and some possibly good news."

No one knew how to respond to that, so we just waited for whatever was coming next.

"The good news," said Ms. Grossman, "is that the big screens seem to be working in spite of the water. The bad news," she continued, "is that the laptops are not working and we have no way of getting in touch with the donor about fixing them."

My stomach did something weird involving a lump of guilt and a glob of nausea.

"So what's the possibly good news?" Steve asked.

"The possibly good news is that we live in Flounder Bay, which is home to some of the smartest computer experts in the country," said Ms. Grossman.

When we looked blank, she said, "Woozle. Woozle employs some of the finest computer minds around. So we asked the tech team there to see if they can get the laptops working again. Clever, huh? We've arranged to drop them off on Thursday, after they've had a chance to dry out some more. I'll let you know what the Woozle folks say when they've had a look."

She beamed at us and we didn't beam back, for obvious reasons. The nerds at Woozle would be all over those laptops like ants on a jelly doughnut. Our futures would literally be in their overcurious hands.

My stomach flopped and I started planning a sprint to the boys' room.

"In the meantime," said Ms. Grossman, "since there's nothing else for the club to do, I've volunteered you to help the janitors dust the security cameras. You can get started on that next meeting."

chapter

40

HELPING THE JANITORS DUST THE CAMERAS MEANT carrying their long-handled dusters around and waiting next to their ladders (and yes, the Offending Ladder was involved, and yes, I did resent it bitterly) for dust to shower onto our heads and shoulders and make us look like we had industrial-grade dandruff. The dirty looks I got from everyone except Vincent were brutal. I wished I had sunglasses to protect me from the glare of their annoyance along with the dust.

When we finally got away and met up at club headquarters, we looked ghastly. Except Steve, who'd somehow managed to groom before coming downstairs.

"Ms. Grossman told me they dropped the laptops off at Woozle today," he said.

"We have to get them back," said Hoppy. "If those

nerds figure out what they do, it'll be over for us."

"It'll be like a movie where the government scientists capture the friendly alien and try to dissect it," said Steve.

"Or take over the portal to another universe and try to drive tanks through it," said Vincent.

"Those things are both way cooler than our cafeteria footage of senior year," said Nikhil. "But still. It's meant for us, not geeks who ride around on scooters at work. Plus, we still need to find out what happens to us."

"I don't think there's any hardware in those laptops labeled 'From the Future,'" said Andrew. "But I'm guessing that whoever built this stuff used tech that isn't available even to Woozle. Which *will* be obvious when they open them up. Anyone who saw it would want to study it for a while. Which means it's unlikely we'd get them back anytime soon."

"Exactly," I threw in. From what Luke had said, whatever was inside those computers would not look normal to a random techie inspecting for water damage.

No one so much as glanced my way. It was going to be an uphill battle getting back into their good graces. Except Lara's. There was no chance I was ever getting back into her good—or even mildly disgusted—graces. That was a lost cause.

I needed to fix this—or at least go down trying. Which meant thinking big. "We need to get in there," I said. "Into Woozle."

"And what, steal the laptops?" said Nikhil. "Not happening."

"It's not stealing if they're ours to begin with," said Steve.

I threw him a grateful smile for his support, but he was looking at Hoppy, his vice president, for her opinion.

"Speaking of security equipment," she said, "do you know how impossible it would be to get into Woozle and take something? It's not exactly on the same level as sneaking in here."

Which hadn't gone well either time we tried it, everyone seemed to be remembering during the moment of quiet that followed.

"What if we got someone to let us in?" said Lara, ending a moment of quiet for possibly the first time in her life.

"Like who?" said Nikhil.

Hoppy snorted. "Who here *doesn't* have a relative who works at Woozle—besides me?" she said. "Let's have a show of hands."

Only Vincent raised his hand. His parents are lawyers.

"My mom works there," said Andrew.

"Both my parents do," said Nikhil.

"Mine too," said Steve.

"My mom works there and my dad works at Hopkins," said Sonia.

"Seriously?" said Hoppy. "An inter-company marriage?"

Sonia shrugged. "They manage."

"My mom works there too," said Lara, "but there's no way she's letting us take the laptops without permission.

I was thinking that maybe someone knows someone who *would* do that."

Now everyone was sort of looking around at one another and wondering who had a parent laid-back enough to either let us into their workplace knowing we were going to take the laptops or let us in and not notice that we were taking them.

Vincent, who had met my aunt Shannon, finally spoke. "Dude," he said to me, "you owe us."

I did. I knew that. I also knew something no one else there did. Which was the identity of the only person on the planet who might be able to fix the laptops for us, no questions asked. If Shannon could get us into Woozle, maybe Luke could get our futures back.

chapter 41

THE FACT THAT SHANNON ALREADY KNEW ABOUT Prescient and Luke and the equipment was a huge plus. I figured I would e-mail her as soon as I got home, explaining the problem and asking for her help.

But as I was walking home, I had—and this will shock most readers who have been tracking my progress or lack thereof—a Mature Thought. It occurred to me that Shannon might not want me e-mailing her at work about the possibility of letting me and others into her workplace so we could take something without permission. Nor could I call her, since she likely wouldn't want to speak aloud about this type of plan in front of her coworkers either.

But I also didn't have any time to spare. The nerds were probably clustered around their technological jelly doughnuts with their tiny screwdrivers ready even as I raced up the front steps.

"You're an arsenic," said Alice as I entered the front hall.

"What?"

"You," Alice enunciated, "are an argonaut."

"I have no idea what you're saying."

"You got in trouble with the fire department. That's what they call you. An artisan."

"An arsonist? Is that the word you're trying for?"

"That's what I said."

"An arsonist is a person who lights fires. If anything, I'm the opposite of an arsonist. I set off a fire alarm—by accident!—when there was no fire. I'm not an arsonist. You, on the other hand, are a nuisance."

"*You're* a nuisance," Alice said. "And a dork."

If I couldn't call Shannon at work, I could call Luke, I decided when this Alice interlude was over.

"Um, how's your ear?" I asked when he answered his phone.

"I think we're past the real danger," he said. "It's not pulsating anymore."

"Not pulsating is good."

"I think so."

There was some awkward silence. I didn't exactly call my uncle often. Or ever.

"So what's up?" he finally said.

"You heard about the whole fire alarm incident, I'm guessing."

"I did," he said carefully. He may have been trying not to laugh—it was hard to tell on the phone.

"Well, the Prescient laptops got wet because of the sprinklers going off and they stopped working."

"Crap," he said. "They're not built to be waterproof."

I could picture him running his hand through his hair until it stood up, something he did when he was agitated.

"It gets worse," I said.

"How?"

"Ms. Grossman decided that the only people in town smart enough to fix them were—"

"Don't say it," Luke broke in. "Woozle."

"Yup. They brought them over there today."

"Crap," he said again. "If those nerds open those things up, they're going to see some stuff they shouldn't."

"I know. I have a plan. It involves Shannon."

"Of course! I'll tell her to get them out and bring them home."

"You can't do that," I said.

"Why not?"

"Because they don't belong to her. She'd be, like, stealing from her own company. Or the school. Or both."

Luke sighed and maybe started doing the hand-hair thing again. "So what do you suggest we do?"

"How many people can you fit in your car?"

chapter
42

BY THE TIME LUKE AND I WERE FINISHED WITH THIS chat, it was past five. Shannon didn't keep regular hours at work, but tonight, Luke had said, she planned to leave right at five—they were going out. Which meant he couldn't overload his compact car with H.A.I.R. Clubbers and head on over to Woozle so his wife could look the other way while we took the laptops back.

I e-mailed the club list with a short message: **Tomorrow afternoon,** it read.

Then I thought about my options. Which included reading about federalism for history, solving for x twenty times in a row for algebra, reading yet another book where someone's beloved pet dies for English, or obsessing about Prescient.

No contest. Then it occurred to me that if I couldn't

question the help screen about whether it was Alice, I could question Alice about whether she was the help screen.

You're either laughing at me or weeping quietly, I'm sure, but bear with me a moment before you judge. Obviously, Alice didn't know now whether she was going to grow up to invent a bunch of security equipment, get the cafeteria footage from my senior year, and figure out how to send the footage and the plans to build the equipment to watch it back in time to our uncle. But surely if she was going to grow up to do something as weird as that, there would be some seeds of it in her six-year-old personality. Some hint of what she was capable of.

That's what I was counting on as I made my approach.

I will present what followed as a simple Q and A (Q being "Question" and A being "Alice").

Q: Hey, Alice.

A: What, dork?

Q: You're smart, right?

A: What do you want?

Q: Just chatting here . . .

A: [no response, turns back to the television]

Q: Do you think you'd ever want to grow
    up to work with computers? You know,
    like Shannon does?

A: [obvious confusion on face because
    computers = dorky, and Shannon =
    cool] I'm going to grow up to be a

famous star who makes up shows and
sings and dances in them. You know
that. Go away.

Q: Well, if you change your mind and
you do grow up to invent some cool
computers, will you do me a favor?

A: No. What?

Q: Will you make your help screens
helpful?

A: No. [cranks up volume on TV and turns
away again, this time for good]

It was clear that Alice had no intention, today, of
growing up to be a computer inventor. But did that mean it
wasn't ever going to happen? Most adults probably aren't
doing the jobs they meant to do when they were six.

The single crumb of information this interview left me
with was that final "No." Did it mean that Alice would
grow up to invent an *un*helpful help screen? And if she did,
would it be because she was always going to, or because I
had just suggested she do the opposite?

It was possible, it seemed to me in a mind-blowing
way, that I had just created Prescient by implying to Alice
that growing up to invent it would annoy me.

That's the problem with the future. Everything you do
has an effect on it, but you never know what kind. It makes
you terrified to do anything. Unless it was you doing nothing that caused your problems . . . See what I mean?

chapter
43

AFTER SCHOOL THE NEXT DAY, AS THE H.A.I.R. CLUB waited for Luke to pick us up and take us to Woozle, I found out that cramming everyone into the car wasn't going to be a problem. Half the club wasn't willing to go.

Excuses varied, but they mostly boiled down to, as Nikhil the Blunt put it:

"This is your problem, Jason, so you can fix it."

The real issue, I thought then and still believe now, is that no one whose parents worked at Woozle wanted to show up there and have to explain. Which left Hoppy, Vincent, and me. Also, oddly, Lara.

"It's my problem too," she said when the others had flaked off, leaving the four of us standing on the curb. "Plus my mother works flex-time; she's already home by now."

"So your uncle is picking us up and your aunt is going to get us into Woozle," Hoppy said as we waited for Luke.

"Yup," I said.

"And they are doing this no questions asked? They're not going to wonder what we're doing there, and why a couple of our backpacks seem heavier on the way out?"

"Ah, not exactly."

"So what, *exactly*, did you tell them?"

Why hadn't I planned for this line of questioning? I gulped, and I felt my Adam's apple travel up and down in my bird neck.

"As much as they need to know," I hedged. "Nothing more."

"And how did you decide what they—"

Here, fortunately, Luke pulled up to the curb.

"It's not going to take four of you, is it?" said Luke when he'd parked the car and I'd made the introductions.

"Hoppy and I are only here to create a diversion," said Vincent.

Which wasn't true. There were zero plans for diversions. There were no real plans of any kind.

"No, we aren't," said Hoppy.

"Sure we are," said Vincent. "Jason and Lara are going to—you know—do the *thing* we need done. And you and I will make sure no one notices them doing it."

"I am not calling attention to myself in any way," said Hoppy.

Luke just looked straight ahead and drove as they continued to argue about this until we got to the Woozle turnoff.

"Here we go!" said Vincent as Luke left the main road and headed up Woozle Way.

"Geez, landscape much?" Hoppy said as the car moved slowly around the gentle curves and over the many speed bumps.

Lara didn't comment—maybe because not commenting was what Lara tended to do, or maybe because she'd been to Woozle before.

I'd never been up Woozle Way, and neither had Vincent or Hoppy. We goggled out the windows like we were arriving at Disney for the first time.

The road wound through bright-green hills and the occasional tuft of ornamental grass or lily-pad-spangled pond. We could see biking/jogging paths meandering across the landscape on either side of the road, but we didn't see any bikers/joggers.

The speed bumps only increased as we drove through the golf course. Luke was going about one mile an hour.

"We could walk faster," I said.

"I think we might actually be going backward," said Vincent.

"My car has low clearance," Luke said huffily.

Then we hit a patch of woods. They were fake woods, though. Well, not fake. The trees were real. But it was more like a garden of trees than actual woods. There was even a raised boardwalk that circled carefully around the individual tree trunks.

"Does anyone else just want to live here?" said Hoppy.

"You can't say that!" said Vincent.

"Why not? Look at this place. It's like Pixar made it. I swear the sky is bluer here."

"But it's treason," said Vincent. "You're a Hopkins."

"It's not like we're rivals," said Hoppy. "We make hairnets. Woozle makes . . ."

"Hypochondriacs," Luke supplied, gunning it to maybe three miles an hour after we cleared another speed bump.

At last we pulled into a parking lot.

"Where's the building?" said Vincent when we'd extracted ourselves from the car and gotten the circulation in our limbs going again.

"Still a ways away," said Luke. "We take a shuttle from here."

"A shuttle?" I said.

"That's not going to make for a quick getaway," said Vincent.

Which is exactly what I'd been thinking, but I said: "We don't need to make a quick getaway. We're not doing anything wrong."

"Technically," said Hoppy.

And now an oversize golf cart was pulling up beside us.

"All aboard!" the guy at the wheel shouted cheerfully.

chapter
44

FEELING MORE LIKE THEME-PARK-GOERS THAN EVER,
we rode up a slight slope, keeping an eye out for the Woozle
building. The golf cart cruised to a halt at a little sign that
said SHUTTLE STOP 1. Where the driver seemed to expect us
to get off. Except we still didn't see a building.

"Is it an underground lair?" Vincent asked.

"They like employees to get off here and walk the rest of
the way," said the driver. "But I can keep going if you want."

"We're in kind of a hurry," said Luke.

"Sure thing!" said the driver.

And away we went, the wind not exactly whipping
through our hair, until finally we saw it, like the Emerald
City shining in the distance. . . .

Not really. Nothing in real life could be that awesome,
especially a place where people go to work every day. But

it was modern and cool looking, with lots of glass panels instead of walls, and small trees growing on the roof.

Again, the guy stopped a ways away from the building (at shuttle stop two), and again Luke negotiated to get us closer. Finally, the guy gave up and drove us right to the front door. "Last stop!" he said.

"Why do they have a shuttle if everyone's supposed to walk?" Vincent asked as we entered the building through tall glass doors and found ourselves in an enormous room that I later learned was called the atrium.

"This place is all about not riding if you can walk," said Luke. "And not walking if you can run." And as he went over to the security desk to get our visitor passes, the rest of us saw what he meant.

There were long people-movers in the atrium—like they have in airports, where people get on a conveyor belt and ride instead of walking with their luggage. But no one was riding on these—they were jogging. Why were they jogging instead of riding? We figured that out when we saw a couple of employees hop on where it said ENTER HERE. They were jogging because they were forced to: The people-mover was moving toward them, rather than away. They had to run in order to keep from being people-moved back where they'd started from.

Luke came over to us. He did not look happy.

"We've got a problem," he said.

"Already?" said Vincent. "Should I pretend to get my foot caught in the people-mover?"

Luke shook his head. "You have to leave your backpacks here. You can't take them with you."

"But where are we going to put the . . . items?" I said.

"I don't know," said Luke. "Let's see what Shannon has to say."

Hoppy grabbed my upper arm and yanked me away from the group. "How much does your uncle know about what we're doing here?" she whispered.

"Don't worry," I said. "He's cool."

She let go of my arm, but she did not look satisfied.

We clipped on our visitor passes and managed to board the people-mover after a few false starts. Vincent almost really got his foot caught in it, no diversion intended.

We all started jogging immediately, and then had to flat-out run to move forward. Nobody wanted to be the one to fall and ride in a humiliating heap away from the others. And none of us did, though Hoppy and I came close a couple of times.

"Shannon's going to meet us in the cafeteria," said Luke when we'd managed to get off the people-mover and catch our breath. "Wait till you see that."

"Yikes!" Vincent summed up our first impression of the cafeteria.

It was large, brightly lit, and cheerful. There were nice smells coming from warming trays and counters and stands. There were sculptural chairs and tables with lots of people sitting around chatting. But all of that was dominated by the "art" on the walls. Which consisted of huge detailed photographs of icky medical conditions.

"Why on earth would they put these pictures up where people eat?" said Hoppy.

"To kill their appetites," said Luke. "They don't want their workers to eat a lot, so . . ."

"Can't they make healthy food instead?" said Vincent.

"Oh, they do," said Luke. "That stuff only looks like normal food. It isn't."

At that moment, Shannon hurried up to us. She kissed Luke. "Hey, kids. How are you? Anyone want a brownie?"

She held out a napkin-wrapped bundle.

Vincent and I both reached out eagerly, but Luke shooed our hands away. "Those things are *not* brownies," he said.

"They look like brownies," said Vincent, his hand moving again in Shannon's direction.

"Brownies require chocolate," said Luke. "And sugar. And butter. None of which are in whatever you want to call those things."

"They're brown, anyway," said Shannon. She studied them. "Brown-ish."

"Brown-*ick*," said Luke.

"You're such a baby!" said Shannon. She turned her attention to me. "Heard about your little adventure with the fire department," she said. "You're getting quite a reputation. Are you going to make the *Flounder Bay Times* again? 'Local Boy in Yet Another Bizarre Encounter with Authorities'?"

"No," I said. "They agreed to keep our names out of the paper."

"I was there too," Lara added quickly.

"You *were*?" said Shannon, right on top of Luke's "*You* were?"

"She was," I said when Lara didn't answer immediately. "Though it was completely my fault." I added this automatically whenever the Incident came up. "Right, Lara?"

Lara remained silent. She was staring out past her hair with an expression I hadn't seen on her before. It wasn't shyness. Or annoyance. It was more like awe. Which was weird. I mean, she'd been to Woozle before. Could it be she was amazed by my blame-taking? It was pretty awe-inspiring.

Finally, she spoke. "Are those the dwarf runes?" she asked Shannon.

chapter
45

SHANNON INSPECTED HER ARMS LIKE SHE HADN'T
noticed any tattoos there before and where did those things
come from?

"They are," she said. "Except that—that's a freckle."

Lara was staring like she'd met an actual Middle-earth
dwarf instead of a classmate's aunt.

Shannon studied Lara for a moment and then said,
"Are you Astrid Andersen's daughter, by any chance?"

Lara nodded.

"Thought so," said Shannon. "Astrid is great. So, so
smart."

She gestured toward a table near a hideous blowup of
what could easily have been some alien disease that made
the victim sprout sentient tentacles. "That table looks private," Shannon said.

We sat down, and Luke started absentmindedly picking apart one of Shannon's "brownies" and then eating the parts.

"There's been a bit of a wrinkle," he said with his mouth full. "No backpacks allowed past reception for visitors."

"Huh," said Shannon. "That is quite a wrinkle. Assuming you guys are planning to leave with more than you came in with."

Hoppy was eyeing Shannon and Luke in turn, clearly still wondering how much they knew about our purpose here. Lara was eyeing Shannon, still awestruck by the tattoos. Vincent was eyeing the remaining "brownie."

"Okay," said Shannon, "here's where we stand. Jorge and Natasha, who are supposed to look at the objects in question, have been tied up since the school brought them in. They haven't had a spare moment to glance at them."

"That's convenient," said Luke.

"Isn't it?" said Shannon. "They'd complain to their boss, but she's the one who scheduled all the extra work for them."

"She's a real hard-hat," said Luke.

"She is," said Shannon.

"Is she you?" Vincent asked Shannon.

"She is indeed. So I think someone could pick the objects in question up without anyone much noticing, but there's really no way you can take them out of the building."

"So what are we supposed to do?" I said. "Flush them down the toilet?"

"Ha!" said Luke. "Not down the low-flow toilets they have here."

"So what *can* we do?" said Hoppy.

"We're going to have to repair them here," said Shannon. "Then we can send them back to the school good as new."

"We have no idea how to repair them," said Vincent. "That's what you people are supposed to be doing, isn't it?"

"Jorge and Natasha can't do it," said Shannon. "They can't even try without seeing way more than they should. Isn't that right?"

The four of us nodded.

"Even the guy who built them doesn't really know what they do, does he?"

Luke shook his head, and Hoppy, Lara, and Vincent noticed.

"But he might be able to fix them, right? If he had a little time and the proper tools?" Shannon went on.

"Oh, he always has the proper tools," said Luke, polishing off his "brownie."

"Wait a minute," said Hoppy. She turned to me. "Your uncle *built* the laptops? And you somehow failed to tell us that?"

For the historical record, Lara's expression had morphed right from meeting-Shannon awe to dealing-with-Jason irritated suspicion.

Even Vincent raised his eyebrows and said, "Dude . . ."

"I just found out!" I said. "Like, a few days ago. I was going to tell you at the next meeting. Seriously—"

"Forget it," said Hoppy. "We'll discuss this later. For now, we need to get the job done."

No one at that table needed security footage from the future to know that Hoppy was going to make a formidable head of Hopkins Hairnets, or maybe the United States, someday. We snapped to attention.

"Wait a sec," said Shannon. "I'll be right back."

She stood up, and Vincent pounced on the remaining "brownie."

"Ew," he said after one bite. "It tastes like mulch."

"Right?" said Luke.

"But not in a bad way, really, once you get used to it," said Vincent, braving another, bigger bite.

"Useless for brownie-glob missing teeth, though," said Luke. "They don't stick right."

"That's a shame," said Vincent, who had seen Luke's trick.

"It really is."

chapter
46

SHANNON RETURNED TO OUR TABLE WITH TWO THINGS: her laptop and a cardboard box full of Woozle-branded merch.

"I'm going to see if I can book a conference room for you guys," she said, opening her laptop. "And these"—she handed me the box—"are some fun souvenirs from your tour of Woozle. You can use the bags to discreetly move moderately sized objects from place to place in the building."

I pulled four tote bags from the box and spread them out on the table.

WOOZLE, they said in big navy letters. And under that: WE KNOW WHAT'S WRONG WITH YOU!

"Huh," I said.

"Yeah, that promo was a major bust," said Shannon. "We've still got a ton of these bags lying around. Also water bottles, baseball caps, pedometers . . . Take what you want."

Who were we to turn up our noses at free stuff? Everyone except Lara crowded around and started filling the totes with swag. We must have looked like we were preparing for a month in the wilderness. Lara shook her head, but she probably had all this stuff at home already.

"Hm," said Shannon, tapping at her keyboard. "I can't find any conference rooms that aren't booked for the next couple hours."

"What about a nap pod?" said Vincent, applying some Woozle lip balm.

I, for one, was fully expecting Shannon to tell him that Woozle nap pods were a myth. But no.

"They go dark as soon as you close the hatch."

"Hatch?" said Vincent. "Can we try one out?"

"Maybe later," said Shannon, at the same time that Hoppy was barking, "No! Stay on topic, Chen."

"Aha," Shannon said. "A lactation room is open all afternoon. That'll be private. And comfy too!"

"What's a lactation room?" Vincent asked.

"For nursing mothers," said Shannon. "They go in there to express—"

"Uh-uh," I said. "No way. What if someone caught us? They'd know right away we have no business in there. It would be like getting caught in the ladies' room!"

"Okay, then," said Shannon. "I guess that brings us to our remaining option."

"Which is . . . ?" said Luke.

"A restroom."

"You can't book a restroom," said Luke. "Can you?"

"Technically, no," said Shannon. "But once you turn the lock it will say 'occupied,' like an airplane bathroom."

"So we're going to sit around in a bathroom watching Luke fix the laptops?" I said.

"Sure," said Shannon. "Why not?"

"I'm not sitting around on any men's room floor," said Hoppy, crossing her arms.

"It's not a men's room," said Shannon. "The Woozle restrooms are agnostic."

"What does that mean?" said Vincent.

"It means anyone can use them," said Lara. "What?" she said in the face of our faces. "My mom works here."

"My mom works at a law firm," said Vincent, "and you don't see me using terms like 'non compos mentis.'"

"You just did," said Hoppy.

"Not in a sentence."

"That was so a sentence."

"But I don't know what it *means*."

I'm going to let the historical record peter out here, mainly because I don't remember how that particular argument ended.

chapter
47

"WHAT'S IBS?" VINCENT ASKED AS WE SAT THERE
on the cold, hard floor of the "occupied" agnostic restroom,
watching Luke open up the back of the first laptop with
a tiny screwdriver. We'd smuggled them from Shannon's
office in two of the swag bags and were feeling pretty
pleased with ourselves.

"Irritable bowel syndrome," Luke said without looking up.

"Irritable. That's not so bad," said Vincent. "Not
as bad as 'angry' bowel syndrome." He was busy putting on his new Woozle cap, wristbands, and pedometer.
He looked like an old guy about to go for a power walk
around his retirement community.

"Is that really a thing?" asked Luke with a worried
edge to his voice.

"No idea," said Vincent. "There's a sign here that says, 'Spending more time in the restroom than at your desk? Check out our IBS info and stop wasting time on waste!'"

"Intrusive much?" said Hoppy.

"The sign about hemorrhoids rhymes," I said. "See? 'Strain leads to pain.'"

"Worth remembering!" said Vincent.

Lara's face was so red it was probably hot to the touch. "Can we not?" she pleaded. And maybe to change the subject, she asked me, "So, what does your aunt do here—for a job, I mean?"

I didn't know, but I went ahead with "Something to do with computers. Nerd stuff."

"Same with my mother," said Lara. "But Shannon's not a nerd. She seems really cool."

"She's a huge nerd," said Luke, carefully laying bits of laptop innard in neat rows on some paper towels from the dispenser. Then he took a few tiny metal doodads (technical term) over to the hand dryer to hold under its stream of warm air.

"I didn't think you could be cool and a nerd at the same time," said Lara.

"I've actually given that some thought," I said. "Shannon somehow manages to be a cool nerd—I have no idea how."

"My mom is pure nerd," said Lara.

"No one thinks their own mother is cool," said Hoppy.

"In fact," I said, "there's probably something actively

wrong with a kid who thinks their own parent is cool. That's not how nature works."

"You mean even a lion cub doesn't think its father—the king of the jungle—is cool?" said Vincent. "I mean, all the other animals must think he's the coolest."

"The lion cub is almost constantly embarrassed by its father's roaring and carrying on," I said. "I guarantee it."

Lara actually laughed at this. "But it's possible," she said, weirdly urgent, "to be both a nerd and cool? Not to your kid, obviously, but to other people?"

"Well, we have one living example, anyway," I said.

Lara looked down at her lap.

Vincent got up to read the many informative signs posted around the large one-stall restroom. Hoppy leaned her head against the wall and closed her eyes. I watched Luke take apart the second laptop and hold various parts of it under the dryer.

"I like science better than playing guitar," Lara said suddenly.

This was starting to get weird. Lara, who never said anything as a general rule, and actively disliked me, let's not forget, was voluntarily having a conversation—with me. Or mostly me, with Vincent now exploring the stall's interior and Hoppy pretty much checked out.

Personal conversations weren't really my thing. Add the girl component and it got worse. Add the shy-girl-who-actively-disliked-me aspect, and it was off the charts. I groped and came up with "That's nice."

Jason Sloan: master of the heart-to-heart.

"I started playing guitar because I thought it would make me cool," said Lara.

I will always be proud of what I did next. Which was nothing. I did not immediately blurt out, "Well, I guess it hasn't kicked in yet," or something like that. Which was definitely my first instinct. Instead, I paused. And I thought. I paused for thought!

Then I said, "Well, judging from the senior-year cafeteria files, it works. You seem cool in them."

"Thanks," said Lara. "But my senior-year self seems to be working so hard at it. Isn't working hard at being cool the opposite of being it? Meeting your aunt today, and seeing her being really cool doing exactly what she wants to do . . ." She fell silent.

Having succeeded so spectacularly with my pause for thought before, I opted for the same tactic again. But Lara didn't need a response from me.

"I'm going to stop guitar lessons," she said. "And join the science team. It's what I'd rather be doing."

"Cool," I said.

chapter
48

IN THE QUIET THAT FOLLOWED, SOMETHING MAJOR occurred to me. If Lara was giving up guitar, then that whole future we had seen on the recording was . . . what? Altered? Gone? This was way beyond Nikhil's mustache. Lara couldn't be forced to be in a band called Lara and the Lariats in five years against her will. Somehow her meeting Shannon today had changed the future.

Hoppy must have been listening the whole time, because her eyes opened and she said to Lara, "You're serious? No guitar? No Lara and the Lariats?"

Lara shook her head. "I wasn't really liking the look of that girl anyway."

"That future-Lara girl?" said Hoppy.

"Yeah. She never talks to anyone; she never even sits down and eats lunch—just hovers by the doorway. She seems kind of . . . I don't know . . . standoffish."

"Isn't that part of being cool?" I said.

"Maybe," said Lara. "If you mainly care about *seeming* cool. But I don't think it's a necessary part of truly *being* cool."

"Getting all philosophical here in the restroom, aren't we?" said Hoppy.

"Sorry," said Lara.

"So what does that do to the future?" said Hoppy. "If you aren't going to be that future-Lara girl, then what happens?"

"I think that future is gone," I said. And hopefully that meant good-bye to the mannerless chucklehead that was future Jason too. I wasn't liking the look of that guy anyway.

"I was asking Lara," said Hoppy.

Lara tucked her hair behind her ear on one side. "I think what happens," she said, "is that I do my best to be a cool scientist, but if I can't, I can't. I'll be an uncool scientist."

"'To thine own self be true,'" I said. This was literally the one Shakespeare quote I knew besides "To be or not to be," which babies are born knowing, and I only knew it because my dad said it a lot.

Lara and Hoppy both looked at me as though I'd sprouted another, better-looking head.

"Very impressive, Sloan," said Hoppy.

I was settling down to bask in that praise for a while,

possibly the rest of the day, when someone knocked sharply on the restroom door.

"Excuse me," said a man's voice from outside. "Security. Are you all right in there?"

The three of us on the floor froze like a little meerkat colony being threatened by whatever threatens meerkats and their colonies.

Luke froze over by the dryer with a tiny and delicate piece of computer resting on his palm.

And Vincent . . . Where was Vincent?

His voice broke the frozen silence. Coming from inside the wheelchair-accessible stall, it echoed as he yelled in the lowest, most manly tone he could:

"Um, yes, sir, I'm fine. I'm just, ah, I have angry bowel syndrome, and my doctor says I can't strain or I'll get hemorrhoids, which could be fatal in my case."

He'd pronounced it "hemorr-hoids," which wasn't right, but maybe the guy outside the restroom didn't know that.

Then again, maybe he did.

"Sir," he said, but not in a tone you'd use if you really believed you were dealing with a full-grown adult sir with genuine bowel trouble, "we've had some complaints about this restroom being occupied for almost an hour. How much longer do you think you'll be?"

Vincent's face appeared from within the stall. He looked at Luke.

Luke held up five fingers.

"Um," said Vincent, his voice not quite as manly as

before, "perhaps five hours? Five more hours should clear this whole situation up."

Luke had one hand over his eyes. He could have been laughing or crying.

"Sir?" said the man. "I'm afraid I'm going to have to come in there. Now."

Chapter 49

THE FACT THAT VINCENT HAD NEVER BEEN AUTHO-rized or encouraged in any way to create a diversion didn't mean he wasn't ready and willing when the chance came up.

Which apparently it had.

"I'm gonna make a run for it," he whispered. And without waiting for a response, he pulled his Woozle cap down, unlocked the restroom door, and launched himself into the hallway. He got a teeny bit of a head start because when he flung the door open, it bonked the security guy. We all heard it.

Hoppy, Lara, and I stood up as Vincent dashed away and the security guy went after him, radioing for backup. No matter what happened next, I knew Vincent would be thrilled to learn he'd caused radioing for backup.

"Un. Believable," said Hoppy, taking time we didn't have to make it two separate words. "But what the heck? Let's each take a separate route and meet outside the main entrance. That'll buy some time, anyway."

Hoppy and Lara ran for it.

I hung back. Maybe because there was a responsible (-ish) adult related to me in the room. Maybe because I didn't love the idea of tearing through the Woozle offices with security on my heels. Maybe because I was still processing what was going on.

"What are you waiting for?" Luke asked.

"I don't know," I said. "Permission?"

"None given," said Luke. "Now get going."

I went.

I pelted out of the restroom and ran down a long, straight corridor that opened onto a vast field of cubicles. I could hear shouting in the distance as additional security guards joined the chase. I ran among the cubicles like a rat in a maze—if the maze had other rats sitting around inside it, hunched in front of computer screens and sipping healthful smoothies.

Workers' heads popped up over cubicle walls as I ran past, but no one made a move to stop me. In fact, I swear I heard some guy say, "Go, kid, go," as I ran by his cube. I zigged and zagged until I saw a red exit sign, which I headed for. Still no one was following—I think all the security types had gone after Vincent, Lara, and Hoppy and were actually ahead of me in this chase rather than behind. Which meant I should slow down? That didn't seem right.

I heaved open a door and found myself in a concrete stairwell. This was the second floor, so I started down, slowly, because I was out of breath and also because I didn't want to take a header on the steps.

At the bottom of the stairs was a door marked *1*. I opened it and found myself at the head of a people-mover, which was coming toward me, unfortunately. I leaped on and, still winded, started running as fast as I could. I felt like I was slogging through a strong current or against a stiff wind, making almost no progress. And here was a security guard now, yelling at me from behind to "Stop! Come back here! I'm not kidding around. . . ."

I've always thought that yelling things at running people like "Stop!" and especially "Come back here!" was stupid. Who in their right mind would obediently halt and then meekly head back upon hearing these commands? It turns out I would, almost. Here was a uniformed adult shouting at me to stop. Ordering me to come back there. Mentioning that he wasn't kidding around. Part of me wanted to do what he said. But only part of me. Less than half, anyway, because I did not stop or go back. I kept running.

My security guy obviously hadn't spent as much time walking the grounds and jogging on the people-movers as he should have. I could hear his heavy panting getting farther and farther behind me. Then I heard him go down hard. I turned long enough to see him begin his ride back to the beginning of the people-mover, then I put on a burst of speed to the end and stumbled off.

I landed back in the atrium. I was stooped over, trying to catch my breath, when first Lara and then Hoppy burst from the hallway opposite me. They were people-moving in the right direction (for them—the wrong direction for Woozle employees), and they were barely winded when they got to me. Way down near the end of the people-mover the girls had just gotten off hovered two security guards, unwilling to get on it going the unauthorized way.

"Let's get out of here," Hoppy said as the guards dithered.

"Where's Vincent?" I asked.

"He should have been ahead of us," said Hoppy.

I hoped he wasn't already in custody. Knowing Vincent, he'd crack immediately.

The guards at the ends of both people-movers were now yelling at the desk attendant, confusing the poor guy into immobility. And then all three guards were on the people-movers, one churning slowly toward us, the other two coming more quickly.

We couldn't wait for Vincent. We ran for the main exit.

chapter
50

HOPPY, LARA, AND I EMERGED ONTO THE WALKWAY
outside Woozle and looked around for Vincent. There were
a few shrubs he wasn't hiding behind, and two of those
overgrown golf carts parked along the curb, empty.

"He must have headed for the parking lot already," I
said. Which was putting a lot of faith in Vincent, I know,
but he is my best friend.

Hoppy and Lara nodded, and we started walking.

As we passed the golf carts, we heard a noise. And that
noise was *"Pssst!"*

"No," said Hoppy.

But yes. Vincent was crouched in the driver's seat of
the lead golf cart. "Jump in," he said, sitting up straight.
"The keys are in it."

None of us "jumped in."

"Get out of there," Hoppy ordered Vincent.

"You don't know how to drive," I said on top of her.

Vincent chose to respond to me only. "It's a big golf cart," he said. "How hard can it be?" He turned the key in the ignition, and the engine started purring cooperatively.

Meanwhile, the two security guards who had been chasing Lara and Hoppy emerged from the building. The one chasing me was probably still on the people-mover, farther back than he'd been before. Stomping toward us grimly were a tall, burly guard and a smaller, more sidekick-looking guard.

What could we do?

There were several things we could have done, none of them involving stealing a golf cart. But Vincent had already managed to shift the thing into drive, and it was starting to roll. Hoppy, Lara, and I scrambled aboard, and Lara actually told Vincent to "Floor it!"

I guess he did floor it, because we all lurched backward under the tiny g-force for a second. But "high speed" and "golf cart" are words you never see together for a reason. We pulled away from the curb and then started to putter along the lane at a leisurely-golf-outing pace.

Any healthy and toned Woozle employee who used the backward people-movers every day could have easily run alongside us and kept up a conversation at the same time. But the guards didn't seem eager to chase the runaway cart on foot. They climbed into the other one and started puttering along after us, yelling something we couldn't really hear but was probably along the lines of "Stop!" and "Come back here!" and "We're not kidding around!" The big one kept his original grim expression, but the small one was getting red and shiny in the face.

Picture the most ridiculous low-speed chase you can. Then add one inexperienced driver (Vincent), one extremely critical passenger-seat occupant (Hoppy), two—let's be honest—sort-of-thrilled backseat passengers (Lara and Jason), two yelling uniformed men (Burly and Sidekick), and multiple speed bumps. I don't know how long it would have gone on—both parties moving at top velocity (= slow), always about the same distance apart—if Hoppy hadn't told Vincent to "Hurry up!" and Vincent hadn't reached the golf course portion of our drive at the same time.

"I'm going to off-road it," Vincent announced, and he jerked the steering wheel and headed out onto the impossibly smooth green grass of the Woozle golf course.

"They're going to follow us, you know," said Hoppy. "They're in a golf cart too, you realize."

"I think I can lose them," said Vincent.

And then he got to say something in real life that most nerds only dream of. He said it in the perfect tone, with the exact right amount of seriousness. I'm just glad I was there to hear it.

"Evasive maneuvers!" Vincent cried.

• • •

Vincent's family went on vacation every summer and did a lot of things that they would never do at home. Among these are zip-lining, white-water rafting, and racing go-carts. Vincent's sister, Karen, was actually the family go-cart champion, but Vincent had been getting good over the years. And now that hard work paid off.

Unlike the guards chasing us, Vincent was not afraid to take sharp corners around water and sand. He also wasn't worried about chewing up the grass, which the guards likely were. So it was on the golf course that we managed to put distance between us and our pursuers. Lara and I could only hang on for dear life as we swerved around golf hazards and bumped over some low hills. We screamed a few times, when it really felt as if one or both of us was about to be launched out the cart's open sides.

Meanwhile, Hoppy was yelling a steady stream of things at Vincent that will not be repeated in this official history. Fill in whatever you want—it was worse. Hoppy knew some interesting terms, and I think she was making up some new combinations on the spot.

Finally, we reached the tree line at the far side of the golf course, and Vincent applied the brakes for what felt like the first time. Hard.

"Where are the guards?" he asked when we'd come to a violent stop and Hoppy was taking a breath between tirades and Lara and I were checking for scrapes and bruises.

"I don't see them," I said, peering behind us.

"We should get out and head into the woods," said Vincent. "We can hide there."

I waited for Hoppy to object, because that was the dynamic between her and Vincent today.

"Let's go," she said instead.

Chapter
51

THE WOODS BESIDE THE WOOZLE GOLF COURSE weren't real woods, you will recall. They were a collection of carefully pruned and maintained trees with a boardwalk and jogging trails winding around them at a respectful distance. There wasn't a lot of cover in here for fugitives, is what I'm saying. We kept off the trails, trotting after Vincent, who sure looked like he knew where he was going, though I knew then and he admitted later that he didn't.

It was easy to move around even off the trails—no fallen logs or half-buried rocks or thornbushes here in Woozle's Hundred Acre Wood. Just soft, fragrant pine needles and the occasional tasteful fern clump. But the four of us soon ran out of steam. We halted, panting. We could see the golf course in the distance, and the abandoned golf cart. The second cart was parked behind it. The mismatched guards were standing next to it.

Remember that scene in *The Fellowship of the Ring* movie where the hobbits are hiding from the Black Rider in the woods? They are down below the road in a gully or something, and he (it?) is standing right above them in those huge otherworldly boots, not seeing them. I was thinking about that scene when I said, "Maybe we could stop running and hide under the boardwalk till they go past."

"Like the hobbits," said Vincent immediately.

"Maybe we could live under there like trolls," Hoppy grumbled. But she was already ducking beneath the boardwalk and taking a seat on the slightly damp ground.

The rest of us followed.

"I would like to point out," said Hoppy when we'd settled into a cramped cluster behind a screen of ferns, "that we would probably be in no actual trouble at all if we'd just run from the building and kept going. On foot. Without stealing a golf cart."

We could see the truth of that, of course. In hindsight. The four of us sat there, feeling the damp creep into the seats of our pants (at least I assume I wasn't the only one feeling that), reviewing our recent actions and decisions.

I know Vincent felt the unspoken finger of blame pointing in his direction. He was chewing the inside of his cheek and avoiding eye contact. I was also pretty sure Hoppy would speak the finger of blame soon.

"You have to admit, though," said Lara before Hoppy got the chance, "the whole chase thing was kind of awesome."

"Right?" said Vincent.

I glanced at Hoppy. She shrugged. "It kind of was."

"It totally was," I said.

Vincent reached over to give me a low five.

"So what do we do now?" Lara asked. "Sit and wait for them to capture us?"

And here is where it occurred to us that no one was looming, Nazgûl-like, on the boardwalk above, searching for us. There was no yelling, no footsteps, nothing.

No one was chasing us anymore.

"I'll have a look around," I said. I crawled out from under the boardwalk and surreptitiously detached my damp pants from my butt.

I looked around the woods and didn't see any living creatures at all. Did no birds or squirrels live here? Some tame ones, purely for the amusement of the Woozle workers on their nature hikes? Apparently not. I checked out the scene on the golf course. No Burly and Sidekick. No golf carts.

"They're gone," I told the others. "The guards must have taken both carts back to the building."

"Well, that's a bust," said Vincent.

"They got what they wanted," said Hoppy. "Which wasn't us, obviously."

"Huh," Vincent said.

"Are you *disappointed*?" Hoppy asked him.

"A little," Vincent admitted. "Though on the plus side," he added, checking his new Woozle pedometer, "look at all the steps I got in!"

Chapter 52

THE DAMP-PANTS SITUATION, PLUS THE LACK OF BEING chased, brought the others out from under the boardwalk. We sat on the edge of it as if it were a dock, legs dangling over the side.

"I guess we should try to find the parking lot," I said. "Luke might be looking for us there."

We glanced around. The Woozle woods weren't exactly dark and deep, but they were large. None of us was sure where the parking lot was from here.

"Just call your uncle," said Hoppy. "Tell him where we are."

"I don't have a phone," I said. "With me," I added, because Hoppy was giving me the pitying stare that seventh graders with phones gave those without.

"I'll call him, then," she said, her pitying stare turning

into a knowing one. My lie had been too little too late.

"I don't know his number," I said.

Hoppy was on the verge of putting her hands around my scrawny neck and squeezing, when we heard Luke's voice calling from the direction of the golf course. "Jason!" we heard. "Come on out of there. No one's mad . . . anymore."

It turned out we'd been easy to find. Vincent's tire tracks across the golf course were going to keep the Woozle grounds people busy for a while.

We trooped out of the woods and met Luke at the edge of the golf course.

He grabbed me by the back of the neck in his version of an affectionate gesture. "You all okay? No one hurt?"

"We're fine," I said. "Sorry we caused such a, ah . . ."

"Commotion?" Luke offered. "Train wreck? Flaming bag of poop?"

"Yeah."

"No lasting harm done," he said. He grabbed Vincent by the shoulder. Vincent flinched. "Nice diversion, there, Vince," said Luke. "You bought me some valuable time."

"Really?" said Vincent, ignoring the "Vince."

"Sure," said Luke.

"Are the laptops fixed?" asked Hoppy.

"As fixed as I could get them," said Luke. "There may be a few bugs, but they should be good to go."

"And we're really not in trouble?" Lara asked.

"I think Shannon is smoothing things over as we

speak," said Luke. "Let's get out of here, though, in case they change their minds."

When I was a bit younger, my mom and I were in a mother-son book club with a few other mother-son duos. We read kids' books (which all the mothers secretly enjoyed) and talked about them once a month. It sounds awkward, and sometimes it was, but mostly it was interesting, especially when we got into mother-son arguments. The point here (and I am getting to it) is that the mothers always seemed to think that the adults in these kids' books were irresponsible. If the adults had simply stepped up and gotten involved in the kids' troubles, they claimed, a lot of problems could have been avoided.

To which the sons in the group would always respond that if the adults had indeed gotten involved in their kids' problems, the books would have been twelve pages long and super boring.

Which is why it's hard for me to have to record here that it was Shannon who saved our bacon with Woozle.

Luke explained to us as we walked to the parking lot that Shannon had told Woozle security that we weren't responsible for our behavior because we suffered from a syndrome called adventure deficiency syndrome.

"No one at Woozle can resist a diagnosis," Luke said.

Adventure deficiency syndrome, Shannon had lied, was a result of too much screen time and not enough time spent in the outside world. Sufferers had so little adventure in their lives, she told the guards, that when confronted with even the smallest chance of a chase scene, they couldn't resist. She'd invited our group to Woozle to introduce us to the outside world, she said, and it had all gone sideways.

"The guards actually asked her if there was a foundation they could donate to," Luke concluded.

"Is there?" said Vincent.

"There is not," said Luke. "And don't get any ideas."

Shannon was waiting for us at the car with our backpacks and swag bags.

We thanked her for the bacon-saving, and she laughed it off. "Not much happens at Woozle," she said. "The cubedwellers will be talking about this for quite some time. I might have to plant a few adventure deficiency syndrome websites around, just for backup, but that won't take long. It'll be fun!"

Lara, as nerd-struck as ever, looked like she might faint as Shannon handed over her backpack.

My backpack felt weirdly heavy when I picked it up and shoved it into the trunk. I could only hope that Shannon hadn't put a package of "brownies" in there.

chapter
53

THERE WERE NO "BROWNIES" IN MY BACKPACK, I discovered that evening when I decided to at least pretend to do some homework. The extra weight was a laptop.

I had figured that Shannon would hand the Prescient laptops over to the school on Monday, but here was one of them in my backpack. Why hadn't she told me it was there? I wasn't going waste time trying to figure out why she'd done it, though, when it was so convenient that she had. This whole commotion / train wreck / flaming bag of poop had started because I wanted to be alone with a laptop and ask the help screen some questions. And now I was. Which meant I wasn't doing any homework tonight.

It took the laptop longer to power up than it had before. But finally it came to life, and I was confronted with one of those dark screens that mean you didn't shut down the correct way last time and now the computer is angry with you.

Then the error messages began.

The Prescient operating system has encountered a Sudden Aquatic Plunge (S.A.P.) event and needs to reboot,

it told me in that hyperdramatic language of angry computers everywhere.

Be aware that an unavoidable System-wide Loss of Operant Parameters (S.L.O.P.) may occur upon initial reboot, with simultaneous Garbled Linkage of Outmoded Presentation (G.L.O.P.).

Whatever that meant. I wrote it down in case I needed to refer to it later, which is a good thing, because otherwise it wouldn't be included in this history.

To begin Catastrophic Recovery Upload Deployment (C.R.U.D.) program, please press any key.

I pressed *G*, because it was right there in the middle of the keyboard.

Except that one.

What the . . . ?

Just messing with you. C.R.U.D. in progress . . . in progress . . . in progress . . .

I waited as this scrolled by for a couple of minutes.

C.R.U.D. complete. If S.L.O.P. and/or G.L.O.P. occur upon startup, immediately shut down the Prescient system and reboot. Do not try to operate the Prescient system with S.L.O.P. and/or G.L.O.P. in effect. The Prescient system is not reliable under these conditions.

The usual computer gobbledygook, as far as I was concerned. Anyway, the home screen was up now, and I was in business.

Luke had said the laptops were fixed—or as fixed as he could get them. But he didn't know anything about the midnight files. So I decided to have a look at a recent recording. Just to make sure the future hadn't been washed away by the sprinklers.

I pulled up a midnight recording from earlier in the week and let out a big breath. There was the bright and bustling cafeteria, exactly as it should have been. Or would be. Or wouldn't be anymore? Hoppy was standing by the trash cans, overseeing some kid as he nervously separated his recyclables. And there was Sonia with a new boy, both wearing retro gas-station-attendant shirts.

Vincent and I were at our customary table, alone. He was reading a textbook. I was shoveling lunch in and talking with my mouth full, probably about my hopeless crush on Lara. Several tables over were Steve with his lump of hair and Nikhil with his shred of mustache and Andrew in his MIT sweatshirt, along with several other kids. They were all laughing.

And there was Lara, standing in the doorway as usual. Ignoring poor Jason as usual. Cool and aloof and—what? No longer destined to be, right? She hadn't vanished from the recordings, but she might as well have. She wasn't going to happen. Which meant that maybe none of this was going to happen? I could only hope so.

I closed the file and opened the T.W.E.R.P. screen. I had some serious questions for it.

Warning! yelled the screen as soon as I opened it. **S.L.O.P. and G.L.O.P. in effect. Vital filters misapplied. Reboot before proceeding.**

I did not reboot. Booting had taken long enough.

I have a question, I typed.

Hello, Jason, said the screen, calming down. **What do you want to know?**

What, exactly, did I want to know? For the first time since we'd seen our future selves, I couldn't think of a question. I waited so long the screen went dark, and I wiggled the cursor to wake it up.

Finally, I typed in the most obvious question of all:

Can we change the future?

The screen didn't blink.

I certainly hope so, it said. **That's what all this has been about.**

Aha! No more "That does not compute"!

H.A.I.R. Club is about changing the future? Not school security? I typed.

Yeah, right. Security. Great club you have there: watching really high-definition dust bunnies roll around in the empty corridors after school and finding out who wrote "weenies" on the door of the boys' locker room. Of course it's about the future, Jason. H.A.I.R.: Helpful Advance Information Revelation. Or how about Help Avoiding Irrevocable Results? I don't know—I'm not Prescient's acronym expert. It doesn't matter. I knew Steve wouldn't be able to resist a club called H.A.I.R. (Don't tell me—he thought it stood for Hair And Its Relations or something, didn't he?) And I knew if Steve joined, you would too.

chapter
54

I ACTUALLY PUNCHED THE AIR WHEN I READ THAT last sentence. This was the help screen I'd been waiting for. The personal, honest one. Give it a good S.A.P., a little S.L.O.P. and some G.L.O.P., maybe a few misapplied filters, and we were in business.

I typed the obvious follow-up question: **Why did you want me to join H.A.I.R. Club so bad? Were you trying to tell me something?**

The next thing I write here should be "There was a knock on the door." Because that is how interruptions occur in the normal world. Politely, and with some warning. But not in mine. There was no knock on the door. There was just an Alice. In my room. Without warning and not politely.

"It's time for you to come down and watch my show," she announced.

"I can't right now," I said. "I'm doing my homework."

"That's not your homework," she said. "That's not your computer either."

"It's a school computer that I borrowed," I said.

She didn't care. "My show is called *The Adventures of Skunk Boy the Arsenic in Dork Land, Part One.*"

"Sounds terrible. Now, beat it. You're being a pest."

"No, *you're* being a pest," came the usual retort.

"Look, Alice. I don't have time for your stupid show. Someone is trying to torment me from the future." Great. Now *my* filters had been misapplied.

"*You're* tormenting you from the future," Alice muttered as she stomped out of the room.

At least she was gone. I got up and closed the door, then turned back to the computer, which had gone dark again. I moved the cursor, and the screen lit up, filled with single-spaced type. What had I even asked it?

Oh, Jason, it read. What can I say? Okay, here goes. You're never going to see this anyway, so why not? Maybe it will be good for me to get it off my chest.

I know you live in a bubble. Your own little Jason bubble, where everything is about Jason. But please don't label people and assume they're only minor characters in your story. Never assume that about anyone. Take the time to really look at people and really listen to them. And learn their names. Please, please learn their names. Believe me, you are never going to look back on your life and wish you'd paid less attention to others.

I wasn't sure that this last part was all the way true,

because didn't being nosy factor in there somewhere? But okay, point taken. I kept going.

In fact, Jason, since we're being honest here, you are going to look back on your life and wish you'd paid a lot more attention to the shy girl sitting next to you in seventh-grade math. You're going to wish with all your heart that you'd at least learned her actual name and not called her the wrong name—when you spoke to her at all— for two years.

Yikes. This was way beyond help-screen material. And it wasn't Alice speaking to me from the future—that much was clear, at least. This was someone way closer to the situation than Alice was or ever would be. There was really only one person it could have been.

Lara. Lara had created H.A.I.R. Club and sent these files to show me what a mess I was going to be, all because I'd ignored her and called her Laura. For two years, though? Geez, other Jason. At least this time around it had only been a month.

But the help screen wasn't done with me. Far from it. I kept reading.

There's going to come a day, my friend, it told me, when you go to a ninth-grade dance and see that same shy girl walk onto the stage with a new haircut and a new attitude and a guitar slung low, and your jaw is going to drop when her band starts up and you understand what a colossal mistake you've made. You are going to fall and fall hard for her, and you are not going to get back up.

So when you see the recordings of yourself mooning after a fabulous girl who thinks—correctly!—that you are a self-centered chucklehead, I really hope you will understand what I did way too late. Her name is Lara, you fool. *Lara*.

And here is where the lengthy and lecturing answer to whatever question I'd asked finally ended.

I'd ruled out Alice as my tormenter from the future, and now I could rule out Lara too. First, she wasn't the type to call herself "fabulous," in any timeline. And second, she wasn't the type to call me a fool, either, no matter what she silently thought. Plus, how obsessive would you have to be to go to so much trouble to torment some kid who got your name wrong in junior high? Way more obsessive than Lara seemed to be.

Only one person knew me well enough to have written this. Not even Vincent could have done it. Unlikely as it seemed, the author of this filterless rant from the future had to be me, Jason Sloan, H.A.I.R. Club historian.

chapter
55

SO, MY PATHETIC SENIOR-YEAR SELF HAD SOMEHOW
grown up to be a pathetic "entrepreneur" who had managed to send his high school security files back in time to
himself. He had probably worked hard on this for a long
while. All because he had somehow never gotten over a
crush he developed in ninth grade.

Okay, he'd made some valid points about self-
centeredness that I was going to have to consider seriously.
But had he really not met any nice women since high school?
Even with his high-powered career as an entrepreneur?
Maybe future Jason needed to stop chewing on the past
like it was an old wad of gum and get out more. Do some
volunteer work. Take a walk, at the very least.

This alone was enough to think about for the rest of
the weekend. More than enough. The problem was, I knew

that if I turned the computer off and it was able to reboot and take care of its slop and its glop and its filters, the help screen wouldn't be this chatty when I turned it on again. My mind whirred as I considered what else we had wanted to ask. My mind isn't at its best when whirring. Here's what I typed:

What is wrong with Steve's hair?

Ha! said the help screen / future Jason. **There's nothing wrong with Steve's hair. It's as glamorous as ever.**

But while we're on the subject of others (and good for you for asking about someone besides yourself!), there are a few things I might as well say. None of this is going to appear on the T.W.E.R.P. screen anyway. Andrew has made it very clear that only the most essential information will be provided, even if you are alone with it. No clues about who sent the files. No hints about the future. No impassioned pleas like the one I've rewritten about a hundred times. He says we can't mess with the timeline any more than absolutely necessary. He says he's only doing this—against his way better judgment, he keeps reminding me—because we are business partners and mostly because I begged so much it got uncomfortable for him.

Andrew. I stopped reading here to digest this new nugget of information. Andrew was part of this? Of course he was. I'm sure you have been wondering how I, a person with zero interest in or ability with computers, somehow managed to invent Prescient. I would have been wondering the same thing myself if I'd given the question more than half a second of thought. But future Andrew could do it.

I'm pretty sure he was already thinking about it. Although he was only thinking about it because it had happened. Which really confused the situation.

I went back to reading.

Andrew's filters will hide all this. He says you'd actually have to submerge the laptops in water for S.L.O.P. and/or G.L.O.P. to go into action. Then you'd have to ignore his apocalyptic warnings and not reboot. And what are the odds of that happening?

So here goes.

First, Steve. Poor Steve. He should *not* make bets he's not sure he can win. Especially with Hoppy. Maybe if we hadn't drifted apart when I got so hung up on Lara, I could have warned him. Okay, we didn't drift apart. I drove him away with my moping and whining about how I wished I could go back in time and change the way I'd treated Lara. It was completely my fault. So be a better friend to Steve. It's really not that hard.

Second, and very important: Vincent. Vincent's been a true and extremely patient best friend. He has stuck by me through thick and . . . well, thicker. Tell him that dare with Karen ended when she graduated. I'm pretty sure she forgot about it after seventh grade. Make him quit all those clubs and get some rest. Except Crochet Club. He's got a real gift for that. The vest he made me belongs in a museum.

And now Lara. Tell Lara . . . Tell Lara that her eyes are the color of a glacial lake on a cloudless day.

Needless to say, I was not going to do that. Nope. Never.

As for anyone else who's worried about what they see senior

year, they can relax. It's the ones who love what they see who should worry. Who wants to peak in high school?

I wish I could send this advice back in time to you directly, Jason. But I've already asked Andrew to do too much. He had to spend a lot of his Warren carrots on this project, as well as his time. So I'm going to have to hope you figure out the important stuff from the recordings and make better choices than I did. All those glimpses of the future need to do is jostle you a tiny bit off the path you started out on. That should be enough. At least I hope so.

Oh, and one last thing. Be nicer to Alice. It looks like her musical *The Dork Ages* is headed for Broadway.

And then, right on cue, the door banged open, knocking one of my participation trophies off the bookcase.

"Mom says to come see my show. She says you need to support my art."

Alice stalked over to my desk, and her stubby little forefinger poked the power button on the laptop. The screen winked out.

Broadway, huh?

"Okay," I said. "Let's see your show, Alice."

chapter
56

I WAS WALKING TO SCHOOL MONDAY MORNING WHEN
I sensed a car following slowly behind me. This is always
creepy on TV, and it was also creepy in real life. I sped up,
and so did the car. I slowed down, and so did the car. Then
I stopped, getting ready to memorize some creep's license
plate and run.

"Hey, Jason!" said Shannon from the open window of
her car as she pulled over beside me. "How's it going?"

"What are you doing?" I asked. "Besides freaking me
out."

"Sorry!" she said. "I didn't want to startle you by
honking. You appeared to be deep in thought. C'mere."

I went over to the car and peered in the window.

"How did the laptop work?" she asked.

"Fine, I guess," I said.

"Did you find out what you needed to know?"

"Ah, yeah."

"Good. Do you have it with you?"

I did. I wasn't going to let it out of my sight until it was back at H.A.I.R. headquarters.

I nodded, and Shannon put out a hand. "Give it," she said.

"But—"

"I need to turn it over to the school," said Shannon. "Don't worry—no one will look at it. I'll tell them it's all ready to go."

I removed my backpack and took out the laptop. As I handed it over, I asked, "What about the other one?"

"One step ahead of you," she said, pointing to the passenger seat.

There it was. She put mine next to it.

"Thanks!" she said.

Her tires actually squealed as she pulled away from the curb and down the street. If the top had been down, I probably would have heard her laughing maniacally as she sped off.

In answer to your obvious question: Yes, I had tried turning the laptop back on and asking the help screen more questions over the weekend. It did call me a dork one more time—I guess because I was alone with it—but it was definitely done spewing interesting information. Whatever filters had gone missing before were now back in place.

In answer to a question you aren't asking and don't care about: No, Alice's new show was not good. It was as terrible as the others, only longer. Except I do have to admit that her song "It's Never Cool in Dork Land" was kind of stuck in my head. Our parents had been humming it all weekend too.

Lara was hovering near the entrance to school when I got there.

"Hey," I said when I got within *hey*ing distance.

"Hey," she said. She tucked her hair behind an ear on one side. "How was your weekend?" she asked.

"Oh, not bad. Kind of boring, I guess. Yours?"

"Mine too, I guess. Compared to Friday, anyway."

"Yeah, that was wild, wasn't it?"

She nodded. "Fun too." She tucked her hair behind the ear on the other side. I was seeing her whole face at once for possibly the first time. "So, I wanted to apologize for being kind of a jerk to you lately," she said. "About my name and all. I overreacted."

"No, you didn't. I'm sorry I got your name wrong in the first place. I need to learn to pay better attention to people. Or so I've been told."

"That's okay," she said. "I need to learn to speak up more. Or so I've been told."

A vision of that other laptop in Shannon's passenger seat popped into my head. Then a cold trickle of something close to fear made its way down my spine like a raindrop on a windowpane.

"Think the laptops are fixed?" I asked carefully.

Lara's eyes widened for an instant, like a cold drip had landed on the back of her neck. "I'm sure they are," she said. "I mean, I'm guessing they are. Your uncle seemed to know what he was doing."

I nodded. "He does. At least I hope so."

And here the bell rang, and the two of us headed gratefully into school.

We were silent as we walked down the main hall toward math class. It felt like we'd said everything we needed to say.

I'm pretty sure Lara had the other laptop over the weekend.

I'm pretty sure it said some personal stuff to her.

And I'm very sure I will never, ever ask her about it.

Chapter
57

THE WHOLE H.A.I.R. CLUB SAT TOGETHER AT lunch that day for the first time but not the last. We had a lot to discuss, and it couldn't wait for tomorrow's meeting.

Vincent had told the story of our Escape from Woozle multiple times over the weekend in e-mails and on the phone, but he told it again for the whole group in person. He came across as the action hero in his exciting retelling, of course, but he made the rest of us look a lot bolder than we had been, so we let him have it.

Those who had refused to go to Woozle with us—for the historical record: Sonia, Andrew, Nikhil, and Steve—regretted having missed out, which was highly satisfying.

"So the laptops are fixed?" Andrew asked when Vincent was done.

"Yes," Lara and I said at the same time.

"I mean, they should be," I hedged.

Lara took a tiny bite of her sandwich and chewed like she had an overwhelming fear of choking.

"And it was your uncle who built the stuff?" Andrew said.

I nodded.

"But he's not Prescient?"

"Do you mean the company or the adjective?" I asked.

Andrew's expression warned me not to mess with him.

"He's not," I said quickly. "He has no idea what Prescient is. Or about the future files. They contacted him through this online game with rabbits and sent the files somehow—"

"Warren!" said Andrew. "They contacted him through Warren. That's wild. Is that possible? It must be, since they did it. But did they . . . How did they . . . ?"

He was too polite to come right out and ask the obvious. "They paid him in Warren carrots," I said.

Andrew made a whistling sound through his teeth, but he didn't say anything. Andrew had really good filters.

"So we're no closer to knowing who sent us the files or why," said Nikhil.

"Or whether we can change the future," said Steve.

"Nope," said Hoppy. "But we can grill the help screen all we want tomorrow, right?"

Everyone nodded except Lara and me. She was nibbling at an Oreo with great care. I was watching her nibble and staying quiet.

• • •

The next afternoon when I arrived at club headquarters, Lara was carrying her guitar case.

"I thought you were giving that up," I said.

"I am," she said. "I'm giving it to Sonia. She wants to take lessons."

"What?" said Steve, who had just walked in. "You're giving up guitar lessons? And Sonia's starting? What does that do to the future?"

"Changes it, I'm guessing," said Sonia. She'd opened the case and was gazing adoringly at the gleaming guitar in its plush nest.

"But Sonia," I couldn't help saying, "how are you going to manage matching guitar cases for your outfits? That's a lot of cases." Her backpack today was orange, as were her hairband, sweater, and sneakers.

She raised her eyebrows at me, then smiled smugly. "Black goes with everything."

Steve sat down in front of a laptop and pulled up the most recent midnight file. The other H.A.I.R. Clubbers crowded around.

"So will the posters for Lara's band be gone now?" Steve asked, focusing on the cafeteria wall.

"Nope," said Andrew. "If the future files came as a download to Jason's uncle, they aren't going to change because we change our minds. These files are read-only, if you want to look at it that way."

"But doesn't that mean we can't change our minds—or if we do it won't matter?" said Nikhil.

"Nope," said Andrew again. "Changing our minds matters a lot. But it mostly means these files are obsolete. In fact, the minute we saw the first one and recognized ourselves, these files became obsolete. What happens in them isn't going to happen like this anymore, because we're going to respond to what we see, and that will change the future. Cool, huh?"

Maybe it was cool with Andrew, but it was incredibly complicated for me. Here's the thing. In one timeline, I was obsessed with Lara the rocker starting in high school, lost Steve and any other friends I might have had except Vincent (and mostly lost Vincent), grew up to start Prescient with Andrew, basically forced him to send our senior-year security files back in time to our seventh-grade selves, and then what? Sat around and waited to see if life turned out differently? Which it now would, simply because we'd glimpsed our futures and made some decisions to do things differently.

Did I *have* to grow up and start Prescient because I already had? And if I didn't, where did this equipment even come from?

My brain felt like an old rubber-band ball from the back of a desk drawer, with various dried-up, broken ends sticking out. I started to feel as if I couldn't catch my breath.

"Are you okay, Jason?" Sonia asked.

"I think I need to breathe into a paper bag," I managed, remembering my mom's treatment for Luke's attacks.

Sonia pulled out a neatly folded lunch bag and handed it to me.

I took a few breaths from the bag and started to feel better. "Thanks," I said, handing it back.

"Keep it," she said.

chapter
58

WHILE I WAS HUNCHED OVER A PAPER BAG, THE OTHER
club members had moved from the cafeteria recording to
the help screen, peppering it with questions and getting the
standard unhelpful responses.

Finally, Steve lost patience and hammered in all caps,
**WHAT PRODUCT AM I PUTTING ON MY HAIR THAT IS MAKING
IT LOOK LIKE THAT????**

"Steve," Hoppy said calmly when his typing tantrum
led to the help screen's standard

**Sorry! That question is outside the parameters of this sys-
tem.** . . .

and Steve responded with some choice language about
what Prescient could do with its stinking parameters.

"You need to get a grip," Hoppy told him when he was
done. "There's no gel in the world that could make your

hair look like that. We all know this but you."

"It has to be a product," said Steve. "What else could it be? My hair isn't going to look like that in five years without chemical intervention."

Hoppy sighed noisily. "I'll bet you a thousand dollars that it is," she said. "One *thousand* dollars say that no hair product is involved."

"I would take that bet in a second," said Steve, "but I don't happen to have a thousand dollars lying around."

"Okay," said Hoppy, "here's the deal. If it turns out in five years that there is a hair product causing you to look like that, I will pay you a thousand dollars."

"But wait," said Vincent, long an expert on and victim of bets and dares. "Can't Steve stick some glop in his hair when the time comes to win the bet?"

But we knew Steve would never do that, not even for a thousand dollars.

"He won't," said Hoppy. "Will you?"

"No!" said Steve. "Geez. What if it didn't come out?"

Of course, if Steve put something in his hair that wouldn't come out just to win a bet, thereby causing the problem, that would be . . .

But this rubber-band-ball thought was overtaken by a memory. Something about Steve. And Hoppy. And bets . . .

"Don't take it, Steve," I said.

But he wasn't listening to me.

"So what do I give you if you win—not that you will, but for form's sake?" Steve said to Hoppy.

"If I win, meaning it can be proven that no chemical is involved in this situation, you will wear something of my choosing every day of senior year," said Hoppy.

It was clear to everyone in the room—except Steve, crucially—that Hoppy had given this some thought already.

To his credit, Steve did give it some thought of his own. But not enough. "No capes," he said.

"No capes," said Hoppy.

"And nothing that will annoy teachers or get me expelled?"

"Nothing like that."

"Don't do it," I warned again, louder.

Surely that warning wasn't necessary. No one in their right mind would take that bet, would they? But this was Glamorous Steve. Not only was he sure he was right, but he could come to school wearing pink satin toe shoes on Friday, and by Monday half the school would be wearing them, and the other half would have them on back order.

"You've got a bet," said Steve.

They shook hands.

And now, naturally, I remembered what I'd been trying to remember. It was future Jason, via the help screen, who had told me to warn Steve not to make any bets with Hoppy.

This hair bet was based on what we'd seen in the future, though. It couldn't be the same bet that future me had warned against. Could it? Or were some things so destined—by fate or personality or whatever—that they would happen no matter how hard we tried to intervene?

More dried-up rubber bands snapping in my brain. I raised the paper bag again and took a couple of breaths.

"So what do I have to wear?" Steve asked Hoppy. "Or haven't you decided yet?"

"Oh, I think you know what you have to wear," said Hoppy. Her face was a portrait of calm triumph, which was weird, since she wouldn't know if she'd won for five years.

"Good lord," said Vincent after a moment's silence. "What have you done?"

Hoppy folded her arms and smirked. "Vincent knows," she said.

"What does Vincent know?" I asked from inside my bag.

Nikhil and Andrew were trying hard not to laugh. Lara's face was going red. Sonia's eyes were wide with dismay.

Steve was back on last night's recording, focusing as closely on his future self as possible. "Is that what I think it is?" he asked.

And now I saw it too. It was obvious if you knew what to look for. Steve didn't have a product in his hair in the future. He was wearing something on his head. Something manufactured right here in Flounder Bay.

Glamorous Steve was wearing a hairnet.

chapter

59

STEVE TOOK HIS DOWNFALL IN STRIDE. I THINK HE was relieved that his future hair condition wasn't permanent (hair joke!). "It'll spring right back into shape when I take that thing off," he said, over and over again. "My hair is resilient as all get-out." He promised Hoppy he'd wear a hairnet every day senior year without complaint. He even offered to make it into a yearlong social-media event for Hopkins: the Hendrix Hairnet Challenge. Knowing Steve, half the school would be wearing hairnets by the time it was over.

Andrew accepted his future too. We spent several club meetings trying to trick the T.W.E.R.P. screen into spilling some hint about who was behind Prescient, but its filters remained stubbornly in place. As Andrew became less interested in the *who* and more interested in the *how*, though, the rest of the club members began to suspect it was him. Then he started wearing a new, oversize MIT sweatshirt. "I think MIT might be the best place to study the theoretical possibilities of sending digital files back in time," he explained. "Plus the sleeves on my UCSB hoodie are getting short."

And what about the rest of us? Did we accept our futures or defy them? It's kind of a mixed bag, actually.

First, Vincent. One day he arrived at the H.A.I.R. lunch table looking chipper in spite of a black eye. "I have an announcement," he said as he took his usual seat.

"Does it involve whoever punched your face?" Nikhil asked.

"It does, sort of," said Vincent. "Be patient, my impatient friend, and I will explain."

He'd gotten the black eye, he told us, during Ultimate Frisbee the afternoon before, when he had nodded off while standing on the field and been hit in the face with the Frisbee. "While I was sidelined with my ice pack," he told us, "I remembered a piece of wisdom I once read in a bathroom stall. Which was: 'Strain leads to pain.' And I realized that it doesn't apply only to butts."

Those of us who had been in the restroom with Vincent at Woozle nodded because we understood. The rest nodded in case Vincent was losing it and not nodding would rile him.

"So I quit all my clubs except H.A.I.R. and Crochet!"

Vincent said. "And I'm feeling less pain already. Except for the eye. The eye hurts a lot."

"But what about Karen?" I said. "And the dare?"

"Karen can soak her head," he said. "Dares aren't legally binding—I asked my parents. And I saw what would happen if I kept going with all those clubs. It was . . ." He fished for the word he wanted.

"Unsustainable," Andrew supplied.

"I was thinking more 'drool-producing,' but yeah, what Andrew said."

Next, Hoppy. Our second official security assignment came a few weeks after Vincent's revelation. Our mission: to find out who had written "weenies" on the door to the boys' locker room. In no time at all, the crack H.A.I.R. investigation squad discovered that it was the JV field hockey team. Which surprised the boys in the group but not the girls. "The handwriting was too neat to be a boy's," Sonia said.

Later, as we watched the midnight recording for that day, Hoppy sighed so hard that the laptop screen steamed up. "Do you see future me?" she said. "Now I'm making the janitors reorder the recycling bins. I not only look like my mother, I'm as bossy as she is too."

This had been a common rant of Hoppy's for a while now, and it was getting old. Which meant that one of us was going to speak up. One of us in particular.

"What, exactly, is so wrong with being bossy?" Nikhil

asked her. "Someone has to be the boss. And you seem good at it."

Hoppy told Nikhil to take a flying leap, but by lunch the next day she'd had second thoughts. Not about Nikhil taking a flying leap, but about her future bossiness.

"You were right," she told him. "I've been hating the idea of turning into my mother this whole time, but you know what? My mother is the boss of a successful company. Her employees respect her. I'd be proud to turn out like her. So I've decided I'm running for class president next year. Can I count on your votes?"

She said this last part so loudly that kids several tables away nodded obediently.

"You've got my vote," said Nikhil. "I love being right."

Nikhil himself defied his fate so hard that he ended up a cross-country all-star. At lunch the day after he won his third race in a row, Steve asked him what vitamins he'd been taking and if he was willing to share.

"It's not physical," Nikhil told him. "It's mental."

"I can do mental stuff," said Steve. "What, like meditation or something?"

"Nothing like that," said Nikhil. "Okay," he went on, lowering his voice and leaning in, "I'll tell you. But it doesn't go beyond the eight of us, understood?"

Everyone agreed. The weirder and more squirrelly Nikhil got about this, the more interested even us non-athletes were.

"Every time I feel myself getting tired and slowing down," said Nikhil, "I picture something awful chasing me. Something nightmarish."

"An alien with double-hinged jaws that drip acid slime?" said Vincent.

"Worse," Nikhil said. He waited to let the suspense build, which it did. "I picture that mustache from the recordings, the size of a person, coming after me like a giant, disgusting, balding caterpillar. It hasn't failed yet."

And it continued not to fail. Nikhil was interviewed for the school paper and the town paper when he made all-star, but he never revealed his winning strategy to the outside world.

As for Lara, she showed up in math class one morning wearing a T-shirt that said FBUS SCIENCE: THINK LIKE A PROTON AND STAY POSITIVE.

"What?" she said when she caught my eye. "I told you I was joining science club. I'm letting my inner nerd shine."

"That's awesome," I said, though I didn't understand the shirt's joke. Assuming it *was* a joke. "But it's your hair I'm staring at."

She had cut off about a foot of it. It now matched the chin-length style we'd seen on the recordings.

"Oh, right. It was getting in my way in the lab. So I donated it."

"You can donate hair?"

"Well, it has to be a certain length. And, you know . . ." She trailed off politely.

"Don't worry," I told her. "I'm not thinking of trying to donate *my* hair."

"That's probably for the best," she said.

The haircut was cool. The science pun T-shirt was definitely nerdy. She clearly didn't care if people thought she was a nerd. Which made her cool, didn't it—not caring what people thought? It was a conundrum, as Ms. Grossman would say.

You may be wondering if I, Jason, accepted my future and ended up with a crush on Lara, or defied it and ended up with better manners. And what about Sonia? We haven't covered Sonia yet either. I'm going to answer your remaining questions by inviting you to a school dance. Buckle up!

It was the Spring Fling, the first school dance I'd ever been to, and as I stood there in the darkened gym, my jaw did drop. Because up on the stage was a girl I thought I knew. But this girl had a low-slung guitar, a new attitude, and not a hairband in sight.

The lead singer-guitarist for Sonia and the Sonics may have looked familiar, and her outfit (black) did match her guitar case, but she was a huge surprise. Remember how I described Sonia as possibly the most agreeable person I'd ever met? It turned out that the lead singer-guitarist for the Sonics had some complaints. And she wasn't shy about expressing them in song. Many of us close to the stage were hit by flying flecks of spit, and it was *amazing*.

When Sonia came offstage after her set, she was shiny with sweat and excitement. She spotted me and ran over. "That was the most fun I've ever had!" she shouted into my ear.

"You were . . ." I couldn't think of another word. "Amazing. You were so amazing. I might never get over the amazingness!" What was happening to me? Where was my Ms. Grossman–drilled vocabulary when I needed it?

But Sonia didn't mind. She hugged me hard and I hugged her back. Then we separated and she said, "Thanks, Jason. You're kind of amazing yourself."

And my knees got wobbly and my smile got big and stupid, and did I mention that her eyes are the color of a deep forest pool at twilight?

chapter

60

THE LAST MIDNIGHT RECORDING WE SAW, TOWARD
the end of the school year, didn't show lunch period. It
showed us lining up in our caps and gowns in the cafeteria
prior to marching into the auditorium for our graduation
ceremony. We agreed that we looked ridiculous dressed
like that, but we also felt weirdly proud of our obsolete
senior selves. They were marching into a future that no
longer existed, but they looked so excited to be heading
out there.

And when future Steve finally removed the hairnet, ran
his hand through his resilient hair, and put on his graduation cap, we all cheered, onscreen and off.

The day after we saw that recording, the fire department
was once again called to the school. This time it was smoke

that set off the alarm in the basement, not a flailing broom-stick. (I was nowhere near the area at the time, I swear.)

School had just let out when the strobe lights and the whooping noise started up. I was on the sidewalk in front of the building. Vincent and Olaf burst out the main doors at a run, their crochet projects trailing. Olaf's scarf looked like it was meant for a giraffe. Vincent's was more hamster size. Or maybe he was making a wristband. We watched with a gathering crowd as a fire truck roared up and fire-fighters raced inside the building. When they emerged soon after, they did not look pleased. One of them was carrying two melted hunks of plastic. And all of them reeked of skunk.

"Two computers in a basement office overheated," we heard the firefighter with the hunks of plastic tell Ms. Wu. "Completely melted. No other damage, though. Pretty lucky."

"Until we were ambushed by a skunk down there," added another. "Animal Control is on the way."

As the firefighters stripped off their fire- but not skunk-proof coats and pants, a familiar van pulled up and two familiar people hopped out.

"Hey, Skunk Boy," said the woman. "We meet again."

Even Luke couldn't explain what had happened to the Prescient laptops. He figured they must have been pro-grammed to fry themselves after a certain period of time. It probably wasn't a coincidence that it happened right after we got to the end of our senior-year files. The computers were unsalvageable, according to the fire department.

The self-destruction of the laptops meant the end of H.A.I.R. Club. We met for the last time in the basement office, which still smelled faintly of smoke and skunk. Ms. Grossman told us that the school couldn't get in touch with Prescient about replacing the equipment, nor could they afford to install a different brand.

Which brings me to the end of the official history of H.A.I.R. Club. But not quite to the end of the story.

"Ms. Grossman," Vincent said as she was turning to leave club headquarters, "would it be okay if we start another club to replace H.A.I.R.?"

"Of course!" she said. "What did you have in mind?"

"We'll let you know when we have the details," said Vincent. "Thanks!"

"I look forward to hearing what you come up with," said Ms. Grossman.

When she was gone, Nikhil turned to Vincent and said, "I, too, look forward to what you come up with, Vincent. Do continue, please." Which meant that Nikhil thought Vincent was spitballing and didn't have anything in mind. I thought the same. He hadn't said anything to me about another club. But Nikhil and I were wrong.

"Okay," said Vincent. "I was thinking when I saw our melted computers the other day that H.A.I.R. Club was responsible for one of the best times of my life."

"The time we met the skunk?" Sonia asked.

"No. Well, yes. That was good too. But no," said Vincent. "The Great Escape from Woozle was one of the most fun things I've ever done."

"That *was* awesome," said Lara.

"It was," Hoppy agreed.

"I'm still sorry I missed it," said Steve.

"Same," said Sonia.

"It sounded epic," said Andrew longingly.

"So," said Vincent, "what if we start a club where we do stuff like that?"

"Break into companies and try to steal things?" Nikhil asked. But he sounded more intrigued than disapproving.

"Not quite," said Vincent. "But kind of. What if we start a club where we go on adventures like that? With permission, though. Those guards at Woozle obviously need more practice chasing intruders."

"I bet the guards at Hopkins do too," said Hoppy. "We could plan the whole thing out in advance—"

"Like a heist!" said Sonia. "And we could wear black—"

"And study building schematics," Andrew put in.

"We'd need to train for stamina," said Nikhil.

"Um, Nikhil," I said. "Before you get too excited, I need to point out that I was probably low-grade humming the whole time we were in that golf cart."

"You were," said Lara. "When you weren't screaming."

"That's okay," said Nikhil. "To be honest, the humming has sort of grown on me."

"So what should we call the new club?" said Steve.

"Anything but Dweeb Club," said Sonia.

"You heard that too?" I said. "At the first meeting, right? That chucklehead as he was leaving?"

"We all heard it," said Hoppy. "Didn't we?"

"Not me," said Steve.

"That kid totally missed out by quitting, though," I said.

"He wouldn't have learned anything anyway," said Vincent. "Once a chucklehead, always a chucklehead, I say."

I hoped this wasn't true, since I was working really hard at not becoming the self-centered chucklehead Jason I'd seen in the recordings. I didn't talk with my mouth full, at least.

"You know what?" Steve said. "I think we should own it. Let's call it Dweeb Club and see who dares to sign up."

"Not Dweeb Club," said Andrew. "D.W.E.E.B. Club."

"What does it stand for?" Lara asked.

Andrew thought for maybe two seconds. "How about "Daring, Wild, Exciting, Energetic, and Brave Club?" he said.

"Don't 'daring' and 'brave' mean the same thing?" Hoppy asked.

"Let's not overthink it," I said. Then I looked around the smelly janitors' closet at my seven friends and said, "Welcome to D.W.E.E.B. Club!"

Acknowledgments

Seventh grade can be hard, and friends really help, so I want to thank my own junior high Dweeb Club for getting me through it, notably Lisa, Jennifer, Marlene, Holly, and Mary Jo. At least we can laugh about it now!

Many thanks also to Patricia Kinneen, my seventh-grade English teacher, for referring to each of us, at one time or another, as "a gentleman and a scholar" and for giving out A+++s at a time in our lives when we needed all the encouragement we could get.

Ongoing thanks to the critique group (grown-up Dweeb Club) for all the wonderful suggestions and solidarity. I have no idea how people write books on their own, and I'm glad I don't have to try.

My agent, Joan Paquette, may not even remember meeting me and critiquing the first pages of this book at an

SCBWI conference, but she changed my future that day in ways I couldn't have imagined. I'm incredibly grateful for everything she's done for me since.

Thanks again to the folks at Margaret K. McElderry: my editor, Karen Wojtyla, for smoothing out the dried-up-rubber-band ball of a plot; Nicole Fiorica, for cheerful help with pretty much everything; managing editor Bridget Madsen, copy editor Brenna Franzitta, and proofreader Valerie Shea, for paying such close attention; Debra Sfetsios-Conover, for the fun and intriguing jacket design; illustrator Lisa K. Weber, for bringing my club members (and their skunk friend) to adorable life.

Special thanks to Crystal Shelley for her guidance and enthusiasm.

Thanks to the gang at the Silver Unicorn Bookstore, and to all the other indie bookstores out there, for helping get my books into the hands of readers.

Thanks to my colleagues for their friendship and encouragement, and thanks to my online buddies for "boosting!" and otherwise helping to spread the word.

Thanks to my family for their loving support, and apologies to the golfers among them for the fictional golf course damage.

And thanks as ever to Stephen, Clara, Max, and Ruby, for being in my corner and/or climbing all over my bookshelves.

Turn the page for a sneak peek at
The Polter-Ghost Problem

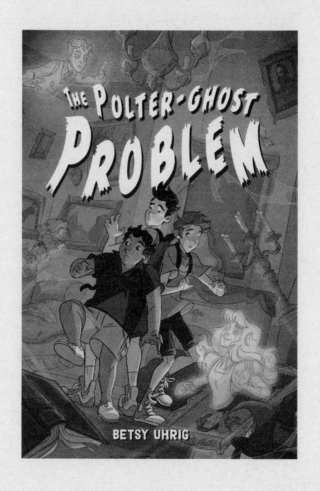

THE HEDGE WAS AS TALL AS the three of us standing on each other's heads. It was also thick and prickly, with the kind of needles that would definitely poke at least one eye if we tried to push our way through the branches. The hedge was growing around a rusty iron fence topped with the kind of spikes that would definitely rip our pants and our underpants if we tried to climb over it. And that was if we were lucky.

We didn't want to picture what would happen if we weren't lucky trying to climb over those spikes.

There didn't seem to be any way past the hedge. Which was frustrating and also confusing. Because all three of us had just seen the strange kid we'd been following pass straight through it, backward, with no trouble. This made the strange kid seem even stranger. And it made us even more curious about what was behind that hedge.

Pen and Jasper, who don't agree on much, both think we should keep moving ahead with the action now so the story will be exciting. But I feel like we need some background about ourselves first so the story will make better sense. And since I'm the one typing, even though all three of us are narrating, I get to decide.

Pen and Jasper read this and told me I don't get to decide and to take the background part out. I said I would, but I didn't. I'm counting on them not rereading and noticing I left it in.

So here's a minimal amount of information about us, some of which probably won't come as a surprise.

There were—and are—three of us: Pen, whose full name is Pen Q. (he swears we'll never know what it stands for) Blaisewell; Jasper, whose full name is Jasper Yi; and me, Aldo Pfefferkuchen (the *P* is silent). We've lived in the town of Frog Lake all our lives, and we (obviously) go to Frog Lake Middle School.

Pen and Jasper have known each other since they were in pre-K together. Pen says Jasper attacked him with a plastic shovel on the first day. Jasper says Pen is mistaken. But Jasper says that a lot. My guess is that Jasper was provoked, which is actually pretty easy to do, so I can see both sides of that argument.

Pen and I met at the Frog Lake Kids' Drama Fest the summer after second grade. My parents were hoping it would make me more outgoing, and Pen's were probably hoping it would make him less outgoing. Pen was a huge hit as the talking candelabra in our musical. I was fourth fork from the left.

When Pen introduced me to Jasper, Jasper thought I was annoying at first. And then for a while after that. But I wore him down eventually.

At this point, Pen, Jasper, and I have been friends long enough to know exactly how to get on each other's nerves—and also exactly when to get quickly back off them. This is the basis of our lasting friendship.

And that's all you need to know about us for now.

WE FIRST SAW AND FOLLOWED THE strange kid who could pass through prickly hedges and tall spiky fences in the middle of July. Pen was back from vacationing in Maine, and Jasper had a sprained wrist and couldn't go to basketball camp, so there we were, bored and getting boreder.

Jasper says "boreder" isn't a word and we can't use it, but Pen and I have overruled him. Pen and I think that if it isn't a word, it should be.

Anyway, we couldn't skateboard because of Jasper's wrist, so we decided to go to the lake. Unfortunately, my revolting older brother, Neil, refused to drive us there because he was "busy" doing nothing, so we walked to the soccer field instead.

On the way, I asked the others what they were writing about for their Frog Lake Middle School summer journals. I hadn't started mine, I still had no idea what I was going to write about, and I was starting to worry. Our English teacher for the coming fall, Ms. Pilcrow, was rumored to be able to tell immediately if you had written your whole summer journal the day before school started—and grade accordingly.

"I'm doing our trip to Maine," said Pen. "There's so much to work with. Pine needles, ocean, rocks . . . lots of rocks. Nature description–type stuff. I've heard Ms. Pilcrow is a sucker for nature description."

"I'm writing about overcoming my wrist injury," said Jasper. "It's going to be a story of triumph in the face of adversity. Ms. Pilcrow is going to be in tears by the end."

"But you haven't overcome your injury," Pen pointed out. "You're here with us because it hasn't been overcome."

"Yet," said Jasper. "It hasn't been overcome *yet*."

Great. Pen and Jasper were well underway with their teacher-catnip journals, and my summer so far had consisted of fighting with Neil and scratching mosquito bites.

When we got to the soccer field, we spent some time kicking the ball around and complaining about the heat and my troll-faced brother and the fact that no one had thought to bring water. We were sitting on the ground, arguing about whether we could suck moisture out of the grass and whether the chemicals that made it green would poison us if we tried, when we noticed the kid. He was standing at the edge of the field, where it met the woods. He had his hands in his pockets, and he was staring at us.

Several things about this kid were strange. We're going to describe them as if we noticed them right away, even though we didn't. First, he had a bad haircut. It looked like someone had chopped his hair off quickly with dull scissors while he squirmed and tried to get away from them. Second, he was wearing shorts made of wool, which is just wrong. Third, he was wearing a sweater. It was full of holes, but they weren't there to make it a hot-weather sweater by providing air vents. They were there because it was ratty. Finally, he was wearing the kind of lace-up shoes that no one wears unless they're trick-or-treating as an accountant.

He stared at us, and we stared at him. Then he started slowly backing into the woods.

Jasper, of course, was the one to stand up. He was the one to start walking toward the kid. He was the one who said, "Are you coming or not?" And after that, Pen and I had to go with him, didn't we?

Following the strange boy didn't seem that risky at the time. It wasn't as if we were following some sketchy grown-up into the woods—he was a kid like us. There were three of us and only one of him. And even though my nauseating brother describes all three of us as "helpless little twerps," Jasper's tall, and Pen insists he's "mightier than the sword," and I'm seriously wiry. So the kid, who was skinny and pasty, would be easy to take, if it came to that. Above all else, we were really, really bored. We'd been arguing about chewing grass.

The kid was partway into the woods by the time we got to the spot where he'd been standing, so we plunged in after him. At least it was shady in there. Really shady. As in darkish.

"Do you see him?" Pen asked, tripping over a root.

"Maybe up ahead?" I asked, tripping over a rock. "That gray blob moving away from us?"

We tried to walk faster, but in addition to roots and rocks, there were tangles of pricker bushes and low branches and even some dangling vines in our way. We lost sight of the kid for a few minutes and were about to give up when he appeared again, closer to us than he'd been before.

"Is he waiting for us?" Pen whispered.

"Maybe," said Jasper.

"He's obviously not running away from us," I said. "If he'd wanted to do that, he could easily have lost us by now."

"So, what, he's taunting us?" Jasper said.

Just then, Jasper let go of a branch he'd been holding out of his own way, and it snapped back and smacked Pen in the forehead.

"I would be," I said, mostly to myself.

Whether it was his plan or not, we were definitely closing in on the kid. We'd gotten used to the gloom and could see him more clearly now: the gray of his shorts and the lighter gray of his sweater. The different-size holes in his sweater. The paleness of his skin and hair.

Did we notice at the time that he didn't seem to be walking in the usual way? We can't remember, but we don't think we did. We probably would have said something about it, something like *Why are that kid's arms and legs not moving when he walks?* or *How can that kid move in a straight line through these woods when we keep tripping and getting snagged on thorns and thwacked by branches?*

We didn't ask questions like these, so we must not have noticed. In our defense, we were busy trying to keep up with him in spite of all the tripping and snagging and thwacking.

We have no idea how long we were in the woods. All we know is that eventually the kid broke free of the trees, and maybe thirty seconds later we did too.

The sun was dazzling when we emerged, and it took a while for our eyes to adjust. When they did, we could see the kid standing maybe twenty yards away from us in front of an enormous hedge, the one we've already described. He was facing us, and as we watched him, he slowly raised a hand in a wave or maybe a salute. His skin and clothing had taken on a greenish tinge from the light filtering through the hedge. At least that's what we assumed at the time.

"Let's go over there," said Jasper.

"We can't," I said. I had recognized the carpet of plants between us and the hedge for personal reasons. "We're wearing shorts, and that's poison ivy."

"He's wearing shorts too," said Pen. "Come on—he's waving at us."

"Maybe he's not allergic to poison ivy," I said. "But I am. I'll be itching for weeks."

Jasper was itching to charge across that poison ivy, I knew. And Pen was always up for making a new friend, eerie or not.

"I'm sorry," I said. "I'm letting you guys down."

Pen waved back at the kid and yelled, "Sorry! Poison ivy!" He pointed dramatically at the ground and then made exaggerated scratching motions.

"Stop that!" I hissed.

"I'm trying to be friendly," said Pen.

"You look like a dork," Jasper said.

"Let's tell him we'll come back later," I said.

But by the time we'd discussed all that, the strange kid, still facing us, was moving through the hedge. His greenish form melted into its depths without a hesitation or a sound.

WE STOOD ON THE EDGE OF the poison-ivy moat, our mouths hanging open. At least I know my mouth was hanging open, because a bug flew into it.

"How—*ptooey*—did he go through there like that?" I asked, spitting out my bug.

We thought about the possibilities.

Then Pen said, "I'm thinking that hedge is actually a hologram. Either that or the kid is a hologram. Or maybe both."

"Why, exactly," said Jasper in his fake-patient voice, "would there be a hologram of a hedge or a kid or both out here in the middle of nowhere, surrounded by poison ivy?"

"Well," Pen began, taking his time, working on his theory as he spoke, "it's probably a secret government headquarters of some kind, where they invent and test holograms, see if they'll fool people. Ingenious."

I was sort of wondering why, if the government was smart enough to do something as complicated as making holograms, it wasn't smart enough to, I don't know, help poor people more, when Jasper came back with "The government? Really?" Which is kind of what I'd been thinking, only not as wordy.

"Or maybe the army," said Pen. "Maybe this is a top-secret army base where they're making hologram soldiers."

"First," said Jasper, no longer bothering with fake patience, "that kid didn't look like a soldier. And second, the army is still run by the government."

"Is not," said Pen.

"Is too."

"Maybe there's a mad scientist's lab behind that hedge," I said, mainly to stop the bickering. "And he's the one making the holograms."

"A mad scientist? Are you serious?"

"Why not? It makes as much sense as the government."

"The army."

"Whatever."

Our voices were getting so high-pitched that the birds

in nearby trees seemed to think we were talking to them, and they joined the discussion, though we couldn't tell whose side they were on.

The real reason we were getting so worked up, of course, is that all three of us were thinking the same thing, deep down inside, and no one wanted to be the one to say it. It was too ridiculous—way more ridiculous than government / army / mad-scientist holograms.

We let the birds carry on the argument for a while, and then I finally said it. "I don't think that kid was a hologram. I think he was a ghost. And so do you."

No one responded. Even the birds went quiet.

My dad is big on "unspoken agreements," the kind where people agree to do something without having to talk about it. My derelict brother is not a fan, which is a source of tension in the family. Anyway, Pen, Jasper, and I made an unspoken agreement as we stood there at the edge of the woods. And it was to turn around and run. As fast as we could. Away from the hedge and its disappearing kid.

We don't need to go into details about what our run back through the trees and roots and rocks and pricker bushes was like, or who fell down, or who ran headfirst into a tree. We all looked pretty bad by the time we tumbled out of the woods, by sheer luck almost right where we'd started at the edge of the soccer field.

Jasper's hair swoop had toppled, and Pen's head had sprouted twiggy twists. I probably looked like someone had turned me upside down and tried to use me as a rake. We were sweaty and we were panting and we were bleeding, and we still didn't have any water. We flopped down on the grass and sweated and panted and bled for a while. Then we sat up.

"So," I said, pulling burrs off my shorts, "if that kid was a ghost—just assuming, for argument's sake—what was he doing? Did he want us to follow him through that hedge? Or was he messing with us, hoping we'd get poison ivy?"

"You don't really hear about ghosts trying to make people itchy," said Jasper. "That's not something they seem to do."

"There are good ghosts and evil ghosts," said Pen matter-of-factly. "An evil ghost probably wouldn't hesitate to give you poison ivy."

"What are you *talking* about?" said Jasper. But this type of blanket objection didn't work on Pen, and Jasper knew that better than anyone. So he changed course. "Giving someone a rash is such a dopey thing to do," he said. "If I were an evil ghost, I wouldn't lure people into poison-ivy patches. I'd lure them into, like, quicksand. And then I'd hang around laughing while they sank."

"You have a point," I said.

"I don't think that kid was an evil ghost, though," said Pen. "I mean, think about it. He waved at us. That seemed friendly."

"So he's a friendly ghost?" Jasper said. "Is his name Casper?"

"Huh?" said Pen, who wasn't allowed to watch cartoons, even really old ones.

"Picture the kid when we first saw him," I said. "Did he look like he wanted to lure us to some kind of doom, even a dopey one like poison ivy? I don't think so."

Pen was nodding. "He didn't look mean," he said. "He looked . . . sad."

We sat there for a while longer, getting thirstier and still bleeding all over our shirts.

"I could really use some water," I said. "And a few dozen bandages."

"Me too," said Pen. "We should go."

The three of us got up and walked toward the sidewalk.

Jasper kicked a pebble. Hard. We watched as the innocent pebble tumbled down a storm drain. We heard the *plop* as it landed.

"You want to go back," Pen said to him.

"Of course I do," said Jasper. "I have a zillion questions about what we saw. Don't you?"

"Yes," I said, "but we can't rush into this."

Jasper heaved a gigantic sigh and looked for another pebble to victimize.

"We don't want to end up with a repeat of the wasp episode," said Pen.

He was referring to the time we'd found a huge wasp nest attached to the back of Jasper's garage. Jasper had insisted it was empty and made us knock it down with sticks. It wasn't empty.

"*Pff,*" said Jasper.

"Or the ice episode," Pen went on. "Remember when you said that the ice on Frog Lake was totally solid, and we almost drowned?"

"No one almost *drowned*," said Jasper.

"Only because of that guy with the ladder!" said Pen.

"How about this?" said Jasper. "We come back tomorrow, when we're prepared."

No one could argue with that.